Alligator Tales

A happy gator!
Credit: Florida State Archives

Alligator Tales

Collected by
Kevin M. McCarthy

Color Photographs by
John Moran

Pineapple Press, Inc.
Sarasota, Florida

Inquiries should be addressed to:
Pineapple Press, Inc.
P.O. Box 3899
Sarasota, Florida 34230

Library of Congress Cataloging in Publication Data

Alligator Tales / collected by Kevin M. McCarthy ; photographs by John Moran. — 1st ed.
     p.   cm.
   Includes bibliographical references.
   ISBN 1-56164-158-8 (pbk. : alk. paper)
   1. Alligators. 2. Alligators—Anecdotes. I. McCarthy, Kevin.
QL666.C925A58   1998
597.98—dc21
       98-20305

       CIP
First Edition
10 9 8 7 6 5 4 3 2 1

Design by Osprey Design Systems, Bradenton, Florida
Printed and bound by Bookcrafters, Chelsea, Michigan

For Marjory Stoneman Douglas
1890-1998
for her work to preserve and
restore the Everglades

Table of Contents ~

Introduction

My fascination with alligators began in 1969, when I moved from alligatorless New Jersey and North Carolina to the University of Florida, which had Lake Alice, teeming with gators, and a penned-up gator mascot in the middle of campus. My "close-up and personal" encounter with the reptile came when I visited environmentalists Jack and Anne Rudloe in the Florida Panhandle, and we went searching for a gator nest.

After traipsing through streams and deep muck for several hours, we found a nest, and it was full of eggs. When we realized that the mother had to be in the vicinity, probably eyeing us hungrily, we quickly left. Because I was following Jack and Anne, I began looking behind me every few steps with much uneasiness. When Jack and I later swam in the Wakulla River, a gator started circling us, either guarding her nest or checking us out for a possible meal.

Another time, when I was setting up my tent by the shores of Lake Okeechobee in southern Florida, I asked the resident park ranger if I had any cause to worry about a gator attack. "No, don't worry about it," he said. "The gators haven't attacked anybody around here, at least not in the last week." That night I slept with a hammer in my hand. I had the farfetched notion of sticking the hammer upright into the mouth of a charging gator, because I knew that then he would not be able to close his wide-open jaw. Farfetched, I know, but it allowed me to get some sleep that night.

Gators have fascinated human beings for several thousand

Gators cavorting with one another.
Credit: Florida State Archives

years. Whenever we in Florida have Northern visitors, the one sight they want to see in our town is a gator, whether swimming in a lake or sunning itself or even watching us at a safe distance. I teach at a university whose football team, "The Fightin' Gators," plays in a stadium nicknamed "The Swamp." Gators are all over town: a beverage company, apartments, a car company, even a shoe repair store. The advantage of having such a mascot is that, unlike the Seminoles or Redskins or Vikings at other schools, we don't have to consider how such a mascot would offend the feelings of gators everywhere in these politically correct days. Luckily, they don't have a lobby trying to rid schools of such mascots.

What follows is a collection of stories about a reptile that fascinates, terrifies, intrigues, and inspires us. I have added some notes at the beginning of each story, whether an explanation of unusual words or a note about the author or even a warning to those whose late-night reading might bring on, if not a "nightgator," at least a mild nightmare. Enjoy the stories and keep a watchful eye when swimming in our fresh-water lakes and rivers. And don't forget the hammer when you sleep next to Lake Okeechobee.

I. Description of Alligators

When visitors come to Florida, they invariably ask to see one particular part of its landscape: the alligator. We residents might try to impress non-Floridians, whether from this country or elsewhere, with manatees and flamingoes and panthers and sharks, but to no avail. "Yes, but show us some gators!" the visitors invariably respond.

What is it about these giant reptiles that has so fascinated people for hundreds, maybe thousands, of years? Could it be their reputation for being such ferocious attackers of almost any other animal that enters its domain? Might it be the danger they pose for dogs and small children? Is it their deceptive presence in calm lakes, just meandering through the water or lolling on a sunny bank, and then darting off to attack their prey? Yes, yes, and yes.

Much alligator literature is either a scientific description of the animals or a comparison between alligators and crocodiles, turtles, lizards, armadillos, or other denizens of the swamp. This collection presents thirty-one selections—some fiction, most nonfiction—that offer a wide-ranging perspective of this most interesting creation of the Southern animal kingdom.

This first section has five different descriptions of alligators: from William Bartram's eighteenth-century portrayal to E.C. Bradford's modern story about the difficulty of getting rid of a dead gator in one's basement, especially when it turns out to be very much alive; and from Hamilton Jay's tall tale about a lovesick gator to Judge E.W. Carswell's pair of mythical stories about Panhandle creatures. ◆━

The Alligators of the St. Johns River
by William Bartram

William Bartram (1739-1828) was an English naturalist who traveled through the Southeastern United States in the 1770s, looking for different species of flora and fauna. He collected rare samples of plants and sent them back to England to a botanist friend. He also sketched the animals and plants he came upon. The following piece is probably the most famous early description of alligators battling each other, as well as a good description of alligator behavior by this famous English visitor.

Bartram's crocodiles, which he mentions at the beginning of the passage, are probably alligators. Here are some terms that Bartram uses that may not be clear to modern readers: verges—*edges;* sedge—*grasslike herbs in marshy places;* fusee—*a friction match with a large head that can burn in the wind;* bark—*a sailing vessel of three or more masts; and* squammae—*thin, scale-like structures.*

This selection is taken from William Bartram's Travels Through North and South Carolina, Georgia, East and West Florida *(London: 1792, pp. 115–128). The very long paragraphs of the original have been made into shorter ones in this edition.*

The evening was temperately cool and calm. The crocodiles began to roar and appear in uncommon numbers along the shores and in the river. I fixed my camp in an open plain, near the utmost projection of the promontory, under the shelter of a large live oak, which stood on the highest part of the ground, and but a few yards from my boat. From this open, high situation, I had a free prospect of the river, which was a matter of no trivial consideration to me, having good reason to dread the subtle attacks of the alligators, who were crowding about my harbour. Having collected a good quantity of wood for the purpose of keeping up a light and smoke during the night, I began to think of preparing my supper, when, upon examining my stores, I found but a scanty provision. I thereupon determined, as the most expeditious way of supplying my necessities, to take my bob and try for some trout. About one hundred yards above my harbour began

William Bartram's drawing of gators, 1773-74.
Credit: Florida State Archives

a cove or bay of the river, out of which opened a large lagoon. The mouth or entrance from the river to it was narrow, but the waters soon after spread and formed a little lake, extending into the marshes: its entrance and shores within I observed to be verged with floating lawns of the pistia and nymphea and other aquatic plants; these I knew were excellent haunts for trout.

The verges and islets of the lagoon were elegantly embellished with flowering plants and shrubs; the laughing coots with wings half spread were tripping over the little coves and hiding themselves in the tufts of grass; young broods of the painted summer teal, skimming the still surface of the waters, and following the watchful parent unconscious of danger, were frequently surprised by the voracious trout; and he, in turn, as often by the subtle greedy alligator. Behold him rushing forth from the flags and reeds. His enormous body swells. His plaited tail brandished high, floats upon the lake. The waters like a cataract descend from his opening jaws. Clouds of smoke issue from his dilated nostrils. The earth trembles with his thunder. When immediately from the opposite coast of the lagoon, emerges from the deep his rival champion. They suddenly dart upon each other. The boiling surface of the lake marks their rapid course, and a terrific conflict commences. They now sink to the bottom folded together in horrid wreaths. The water becomes thick and discoloured. Again they rise, their jaws clap together, re-echoing through the deep surrounding forests. Again they sink, when the contest ends at the muddy bottom of the lake, and the vanquished makes a hazardous escape, hiding himself in the muddy turbulent waters and sedge on a distant shore. The proud victor exulting returns to the place of action. The shores and forests resound his dreadful roar, together with the triumphing shouts of the plaited tribes around, witnesses of the horrid combat.

My apprehensions were highly alarmed after being a spectator of so dreadful a battle. It was obvious that every delay would but tend to encrease [increase] my dangers and difficulties, as the sun was near setting, and the alligators gathered around my harbour from all quarters. From these considerations I concluded to be expeditious in my trip to the lagoon, in order to take some fish. Not thinking it prudent to take my fusee with me, lest I might lose it overboard in case of a battle, which I had every reason to dread before my return, I therefore furnished myself with a club for my defence, went on board, and penetrating the first line of those which surrounded my harbour, they gave way; but being pursued by several very large ones, I kept strictly on the watch, and paddled with all my might towards the entrance of the lagoon, hoping to be sheltered there from the multitude of my assailants; but ere I had half-way reached the place, I was attacked on all sides, several endeavoring to overset the canoe. My situation now became precarious to the last degree: two very large ones attacked me closely, at the same instant, rushing up with their heads and part of their bodies above the water, roaring terribly and belching floods of water over me. They struck their jaws together so close to my ears, as almost to stun me, and I expected every moment to be dragged out of the boat and instantly devoured. But I applied my weapons so effectually about me, though at random, that I was so successful as to beat them off a little; when, finding that they designed to renew the battle, I made for the shore, as the only means left me for my preservation; for, by keeping close to it, I should have my enemies on one side of me only, whereas I was before surrounded by them; and there was a probability, if pushed to the last extremity, of saving myself, by jumping out of the canoe on shore, as it is easy to outwalk them on land, although comparatively as swift as lightning in the water. I found this last expedient alone could fully answer my expectations, for as soon as I gained the shore, they drew off and kept aloof. This was a happy relief, as my confidence was, in some degree, recovered by it.

On recollecting myself, I discovered that I had almost reached the

---

entrance of the lagoon, and determined to venture in, if possible, to take a few fish, and then return to my harbour, while day-light continued; for I could now, with caution and resolution, make my way with safety along shore; and indeed there was no other way to regain my camp, without leaving my boat and making my retreat through the marshes and reeds, which, if I could even effect, would have been in a manner throwing myself away, for then there would have been no hopes of ever recovering my bark, and returning in safety to any settlements of men. I accordingly proceeded, and made good my entrance into the lagoon, though not without opposition from the alligators, who formed a line across the entrance, but did not pursue me into it, nor was I molested by any there, though there were some very large ones in a cove at the upper end. I soon caught more trout than I had present occasion for, and the air was too hot and sultry to admit of their being kept for many hours, even though salted or barbecued.

I now prepared for my return to camp, which I succeeded in with but little trouble, by keeping close to the shore; yet I was opposed upon re-entering the river out of the lagoon, and pursued near to my landing (though not closely attacked), particularly by an old daring one, about twelve feet in length, who kept close after me; and when I stepped on shore and turned about, in order to draw up my canoe, he rushed up near my feet, and lay there for some time, looking me in the face, his head and shoulders out of water. I resolved he should pay for his temerity, and having a heavy load in my fusee, I ran to my camp, and returning with my piece, found him with his foot on the gunwale of the boat, in search of fish. On my coming up he withdrew sullenly and slowly into the water, but soon returned and placed himself in his former position, looking at me, and seeming neither fearful nor any way disturbed. I soon dispatched him by lodging the contents of my gun in his head, and then proceeded to cleanse and prepare my fish for supper; and accordingly took them out of the boat, laid them down on the sand close to the water, and began to scale them; when, raising my head, I saw before me, through the clear water, the head and shoulders of a very large alligator, moving slowly towards me.

I instantly stepped back, when, with a sweep of his tail, he brushed off several of my fish. It was certainly most providential that I looked up at that instant, as the monster would probably, in less than a minute, have seized and dragged me into the river. This incredible boldness of the animal disturbed me greatly, supposing there could now be no reasonable safety for me during the night, but by keeping continually on

Early picture of Indians killing gators, 1591.
Credit: Florida State Archives

the watch: I therefore, as soon as I had prepared the fish, proceeded to secure myself and effects in the best manner I could.

In the first place, I hauled my bark upon the shore, almost clear out of the water, to prevent their oversetting or sinking her; after this, every moveable was taken out and carried to my camp, which was but a few yards off; then ranging some dry wood in such order as was the most convenient, myself I cleared the ground round about it, that there might be no impediment in my way, in case of an attack in the night, either from the water or the land; for I discovered by this time, that this small isthmus, from its remote situation and fruitfulness, was resorted to by bears and wolves.

Having prepared myself in the best manner I could, I charged my gun and proceeded to reconnoitre my camp and the adjacent grounds; when I discovered that the peninsula and grove, at the distance of about two hundred yards from my encampment, on the land side, were invested by a cypress swamp, covered with water, which below was joined to the shore of the little lake, and above to the marshes surrounding the lagoon; so that I was confined to an islet exceedingly circumscribed, and I found there was no other retreat for me, in case of an attack, but by either ascending one of the large oaks, or pushing off with my boat.

It was by this time dusk, and the alligators had nearly ceased their roar, when I was again alarmed by a tumultuous noise that seemed to be in my harbour, and therefore engaged my immediate attention. Returning to my camp, I found it undisturbed, and then continued on to the extreme point of the promontory, where I saw a scene, new and surprising, which at first threw my senses into such a tumult, that it was some time before I could comprehend what was the matter; however, I soon accounted for the prodigious assemblage of crocodiles at this place, which exceeded every thing of the kind I had ever heard of.

How shall I express myself so as to convey an adequate idea of it to the reader, and at the same time avoid raising suspicions of my veracity. Should I say, that the river (in this place) from shore to shore, and perhaps near half a mile above and below me, appeared to be one solid bank of fish, of various kinds, pushing through this narrow pass of St. Juan's into the little lake, on their return down the river, and that the alligators were in such incredible numbers, and so close together from shore to shore, that it would have been easy to have walked across on their heads, had the animals been harmless? What expressions can sufficiently declare the shocking scene that for some minutes continued, whilst this mighty army of fish were forcing the pass?

During this attempt, thousands, I may say hundreds of thousands, of them were caught and swallowed by the devouring alligators. I have seen an alligator take up out of the water several great fish at a time, and just squeeze them betwixt his jaws, while the tails of the great trout flapped about his eyes and lips, ere he had swallowed them. The horrid noise of their closing jaws, their plunging amidst the broken banks of fish, and rising with their prey some feet upright above the water, the floods of water and blood rushing out of their mouths, and the clouds of vapour issuing from their wide nostrils, were truly frightful. This scene continued at intervals during the night, as the fish came to the pass. After this fight, shocking and tremendous as it was, I found myself somewhat easier and more reconciled to my situation; being convinced that their extraordinary assemblage here was owing to this annual feast of fish; and that they were so well employed in their own element, that I had little occasion to fear their paying me a visit.

It being now almost night, I returned to my camp, where I had left my fish broiling, and my kettle of rice stewing; and having with me oil, pepper, and salt, and excellent oranges hanging in abundance over my head (a valuable substitute for vinegar) I sat down and regaled myself cheerfully. Having finished my repast, I rekindled my fire for light, and whilst I was revising the notes of my past day's journey, I was suddenly roused with a noise behind me toward the main land. I sprang up on my feet, and listening, I distinctly heard some creature wading in the water of the isthmus. I seized my gun and went cautiously from my camp, directing my steps towards the noise: when I had advanced about thirty yards, I halted behind a coppice of orange trees, and soon perceived two very large bears, which had made their way through the water, and had landed in the grove, about one hundred yards distance from me, and were advancing towards me. I waited until they were within thirty yards of me: they there began to snuff and look towards my camp: I snapped my piece, but it flashed, on which they both turned about and galloped off, plunging through the water and swamp, never halting, as I suppose, until they reached fast land, as I could hear them leaping and plunging a long time. They did not presume to return again, nor was I molested by any other creature, except being occasionally awakened by the whooping of owls, screaming of bitterns, or the wood-rats running amongst the leaves.

* * *

The noise of the crocodiles kept me awake the greater part of the night; but when I arose in the morning, contrary to my expectations, there was perfect peace; very few of them to be seen, and those were asleep on the shore. Yet I was not able to suppress my fears and apprehensions of being attacked by them in future; and indeed yesterday's combat with them, notwithstanding I came off in a manner victorious, or at least made a safe retreat, had left sufficient impression on my mind to damp my courage; and it seemed too much for one of my strength, being alone in a very small boat, to encounter such collected danger. To pursue my voyage up the river, and be obliged every evening to pass such dangerous defiles, appeared to me as perilous as running the gauntlet betwixt two rows of Indians armed with knives and fire-brands. I however resolved to continue my voyage one day longer, if I possibly could with safety, and then return down the river, should I find the like difficulties to oppose. Accordingly I got every thing on board, charged my gun, and set sail cautiously, along shore.

As I passed by Battle lagoon, I began to tremble and keep a good look out; when suddenly a huge alligator rushed out of the reeds, and with a tremendous roar came up, and darted as swift as an arrow under my boat, emerging upright on my lee quarter, with open jaws, and belching water and smoke that fell upon me like rain in a hurricane. I laid soundly about his head with my club and beat him off; and after plunging and darting about my boat, he went off on a straight line through the water, seemingly with the rapidity of lightning, and entered the cape of the lagoon. I now employed my time to the very best advantage in paddling close along shore, but could not forbear looking now and then behind me, and presently perceived one of them coming up again.

The water of the river hereabouts was shoal and very clear; the monster came up with the usual roar and menaces, and passed close by the side of my boat, when I could distinctly see a young brood of alligators, to the number of one hundred or more, following after her in a long train. They kept close together in a column without straggling off to the one side or the other; the young appeared to be of an equal size, about fifteen inches in length, almost black, with pale yellow transverse waved clouds or blotches, much like rattlesnakes in colour. I now lost sight of my enemy again.

Still keeping close along shore, on turning a point or projection of the river bank, at once I beheld a great number of hillocks or small pyramids, resembling hay-cocks, ranged like an encampment along the banks. They stood fifteen or twenty yards distant from the water, on a high marsh, about four feet perpendicular above the water. I knew them to be the nests of the crocodile, having had a description of them before; and now expected a furious and general attack, as I saw several large crocodiles swimming abreast of these buildings. These nests being so great a curiosity to me, I was determined at all events immediately to land and examine them. Accordingly, I ran my bark on shore at one of their landing-places, which was a sort of nick or little dock, from which ascended a sloping path or road up to the edge of the meadow, where their nests were; most of them were deserted, and the great thick whitish egg-shells lay broken and scattered upon the ground round about them.

The nests or hillocks are of the form of an obtuse cone, four feet high and four or five feet in diameter at their bases; they are constructed with mud, grass, and herbage. At first they lay a floor of this kind of tempered mortar on the ground, upon which they deposit a layer of eggs, and upon this a stratum of mortar seven or eight inches in thickness, and then another layer of eggs, and in this manner one stratum upon another, nearly to the top. I believe they commonly lay from one to two hundred eggs in a nest: these are hatched, I suppose, by the heat of the sun; and perhaps the vegetable substances mixed with the earth, being acted upon by the sun, may cause a small degree of fermentation, and so increase the heat in those hillocks. The ground for several acres about these nests shewed [showed] evident marks of a continual resort of alligators; the grass was every where beaten down, hardly a blade or straw was left standing; whereas, all about, at a distance, it was five or six feet high, and as thick as it could grow together.

The female, as I imagine, carefully watches her own nest of eggs until they are all hatched; or perhaps while she is attending her own brood, she takes under her care and protection as many as she can get at one time, either from her own particular nest or others: but certain it is, that the young are not left to shift for themselves; for I have had frequent opportunities of seeing the female alligator leading about the shores her train of young ones, just as a hen does her brood of chickens; and she is equally assiduous and courageous in defending the young, which are under her care, and providing for their subsistence; and when she is basking upon the warm banks, with her brood around her, you may hear the young ones continually whining and barking, like young puppies. I believe but few of a brood live to the years of full growth and magnitude, as the old feed on the young as long as they can make prey of them.

The alligator when full grown is a very large and terrible creature, and of prodigious strength, activity, and swiftness in the water. I have seen them twenty feet in length, and some are supposed to be twenty-two or twenty-three feet. Their body is as large as that of a horse; their shape exactly resembles that of a lizard, except their tail, which is flat or cuneiform, being compressed on each side, and gradually diminishing from the abdomen to the extremity, which, with the whole body is covered with horny plates or squammae, impenetrable when on the body of the live animal, even to a rifle ball, except about their head and just behind their fore-legs or arms, where it is said they are only vulnerable. The head of a full grown one is about three feet, and the mouth opens nearly the same length; their eyes are small in proportion and seem sunk deep in the head, by means of the prominency of the brows; the nostrils are large, inflated and prominent on the top, so that the head in the water resembles, at a distance, a great chunk of wood floating about.

Only the upper jaw moves, which they raise almost perpendicular, so as to form a right angle with the lower one. In the fore-part of the upper jaw, on each side, just under the nostrils, are two very large, thick, strong teeth or tusks, not very sharp, but rather the shape of a cone: these are as white as the finest polished ivory, and are not covered by any skin or lips, and always in sight, which gives the creature a frightful appearance: in the lower jaw are holes opposite to these teeth, to receive them: when they clap their jaws together it causes a surprising noise, like that which is made by forcing a heavy plank with violence upon the ground, and may be heard at a great distance.

But what is yet more surprising to a stranger, is the incredible loud and terrifying roar, which they are capable of making, especially in the spring season, their breeding time. It most resembles very heavy distant thunder, not only shaking the air and waters, but causing the earth to tremble; and when hundreds and thousands are roaring at the same time, you can scarcely be persuaded, but that the whole globe is violently and dangerously agitated.

An old champion, who is perhaps absolute sovereign of a little lake or lagoon (when fifty less than himself are obliged to content themselves with swelling and roaring in little coves round about) darts forth from the reedy coverts all at once, on the surface of the waters, in a right line; at first seemingly as rapid as lightning, but gradually more slowly until he arrives at the center of the lake, when he stops. He now swells himself by drawing in wind and water through his mouth, which causes a loud sonorous rattling in the throat for near a minute, but it is immediately forced out again through his mouth and nostrils, with a loud noise, brandishing his tail in the air, and the vapour ascending from his nostrils like smoke. At other times, when swollen to an extent ready to burst, his head and tail lifted up, he spins or twirls round on the surface of the water. He acts his part like an Indian chief when rehearsing his feats of war; and then retiring, the exhibition is continued by others who dare to step forth, and strive to excel each other, to gain the attention of the favourite female.

Some Florida Alligators
by Hamilton Jay

In this tall tale about a lovesick gator and another grateful one, several terms need explaining: laving—*washing;* demmyjohn *or* demijohn—*a narrow-necked jug;* mashed—*became smitten with affection for someone;* toney—*high-minded, elitist; and* ipecac—*a medicine used to induce vomiting. Hamilton Jay was a popular writer of the nineteenth century, especially in newspapers. This story appeared in* The Eustis Lake Region *(Eustis, Florida, July 26, 1888).*

C *rocidilus lucius,*" said the professor, sipping his gin reflectively, and moving his hat away from the angle of the major's expectoration. "*Saurian carnirivorous* came from *carne*, meat, and *rivorous*, a river. Mighty big river meat an alligator is, too. When you are laving in the aqueous element, and see a twenty-foot alligator approaching you, the impression it produces in your mind is, to say the least of it, somewhat depressing. And yet the alligator is one of the most intelligent of the amphibious tribe, and susceptible of a very high degree of education. How wonderful are thy works, O Nature."

"Yes, and you're about the most won'fnl," said the major sarcastically, "and if that there demmyjohn was shoved a leetle nearer this way, some of the rest of us might have a pull at it onct [once] in a while. Not that I object to your having all that you can get, for I know your wire grass stummick is right smart dry, but manners is manners the world over, and the judge here has barely wet his lips yet. Don't you see the smoke coming out of his ears?"

There was a general laugh at this sally, and the portly corn-fed judge took advantage of the confusion to absorb about a stick full of the best gin that ever retailed for one dollar a gallon.

"Talking about 'gators," said the colonel, gazing thoughtfully at his empty glass, "the professor is right. 'Gators can be trained to do most anything, and are a heap sight more trustworthy than some . . . men . . . I know. D'ye remember when I was keeping hotel on the Indian River, Judge?"

A wary gator keeps an eye on the photographer.
Credit: Florida State Archives

"I should say I did," said the Judge. "I took dinner there once and it cost me nine bottles of Dr. Pepsin's curious cure to get over it."

"Oh, it did, did it? Well, Judge, since you are so very smart, perhaps you can tell me the difference between recollect and remember. No? Well, I'll tell you, Judge. I recollect that you took dinner there with me, but I don't remember that you ever paid for it."

The laugh was on the judge, but he took it good naturedly and remarked, "Well, I'll pay for it now, Colonel, in drinks all around. Here, Jo, bring in the red licker and don't put any water in it either. Water," he added reflectively, "was not intended as a beverage, for the Good Book only mentions it once in that connection and that was by Dives and he was in hell when he asked for it. But go on with your story, Colonel."

"Well," said the colonel, taking a fresh quid of tobacco, "when I was keeping hotel I had an eight-foot 'gator that was a heap smarter than any [black man] I ever seen. I got him when he was about a month old,

Alligators can be taught to do tricks.
Credit: Florida State Archives

and trained him up in the way he should go, walking that way occasionally myself to sorter encourage him like. As he growed up, he was very handy about the house, helping the women folks hang out clothes, bringing wood into the kitchen, cleaning fish and such like work.

"Lots of Yankees used to be down here in the winter, and they were much interested in Henry, which was the name of the 'gator. One day as one of these fellows was paying his bill and leaving, he turned to me and said: 'Colonel, if I was you, I'd make a head waiter out of Henry....'

"Well, gentlemen, that suggestion just naturally ha[u]nted me, and when the dull summer set in, I put the 'gator through a course of training that would have surprised you, and when the season opened, I was ready. The hotel was crowded the first week, had to turn folks away. I had the 'gator dressed up in a broadcloth suit, swallow tail coat, white vest, standing collar, white cravat, and patent leather slippers. He was the best head waiter I ever had, and a perfect gentleman. The little children said he smiled just like a Sunday school superintendent. He could uncork a bottle of wine as handy as I can, and none of the other waiters dared neglect their duties. He'd just grate his teeth a little and they'd move around as spry as a tax collector. He used to pick up lots of quarters, and as he was liberal in treating, he was well liked by all the 'boys,' poor fellow."

He paused and wiped a tear off the tip of his rubicund nose.

"What became of him, Colonel?" they asked in chorus.

"Poor fellow, he got mashed on a pretty girl from New York who was stopping at the hotel, and followed her all around. Of course, she was too toney to have anything to do with a 'gator, even an educated one, tho' she might have done worse. She reported the matter to me and I tried to reason with Henry, but he wouldn't have it, so I put him back in the kitchen. He took to drinking after that, and finally committed suicide in his room over the kitchen; shot himself through the heart with a derringer I'd given him the Christmas before. He left a note stating he was tired of life, and requested that I cut up his body and feed it to the hogs, and that his teeth be made into a necklace for the young lady aforesaid."

"Did you comply with this last will and testament?" said the major.

"I did, sir," replied the colonel, reaching out for the whisky bottle and helping himself to a second mate's drink.

"And all liars shall have their place in the lake of fire and brimstone," said the professor, musingly.

"Gentlemen, did you ever know that I once practiced medicine?" said the judge, mildly.

"Well, not exactly," said the professor, "but I thought you had from the looks of that cemetery back of your plantation."

The colonel and the judge laughed so heartily that they didn't see how big a drink the major was taking.

"Yes, siree, Bob, I was a regular full feathered M.D.," resumed the judge, "and an incident in my practice gave me a very exalted opinion of the gratitude of dumb animals.

"One day I was wandering along a lonely part of the road near Eustis, Lake County, when my horse shied and then turned clear around and refused to go forward. I dismounted, tied [the horse] to a sapling and started ahead to see what was up. Just around the bend of the road was the biggest 'gator I ever saw since peace broke out. It was all of 18 foot long, and had a head as big as a flour barrel. I saw it was helpless, and was about to shoot it, when it gave me such an appealing look that I put my pistol back in my pocket and drew nearer to the suffering critter. It seemed to be in great misery, and heaved groans as if it had eaten something that disagreed with it mightily. It didn't seem to have a bit of fear of me, but groaned and eyed my medicine case wistfully. A

Don't try this at home.
Credit: Florida State Archives

bright idea struck me. I had a package of ipecac with me, and I took it out and chucked it in the 'gator's mouth. In a little while the fun commenced. The 'gator histed up his shoulders, gave a big retch, and up and out came about four pounds of bologny sausage, four pine knots and the upper part of a Dutch pedlar. This relieved him, and in a little while he was able to move off to the water.

"Well, sir, about three months after that I was sent for to attend Jim Fergerson's wife, who was suffering from ensymosis of the sespedal artery. I got about halfway there when my horse stumbled and lamed himself so badly I didn't dare ride him any further. I tied him up and went along on foot. When I got to the slew, I found the water up, so I knew I couldn't ford it, and there I was up a tree, so to speak. While I was study-ing what to do, I heard a rustling in the bushes, and there was the old 'gator I had relieved of an overburdened stomach. He looked at me and then at the slew, and seemed to grasp the situation in a minute. He winked at me as if to say, 'I'll get you out of this, old pardner,' and then gave a shrill whistle. In a minute the slew was alive with 'gators. My friend swam out to them, and soon I saw them range in side by side, hump their backs up out of the water, and there was a firm bridge over which I walked across to the other side. I found the old woman very sick, but applied a hot poultice to the ulterior process, and left her doing all right. When I got back to the slew, the 'gators formed the bridge again, and I got safely home. Now that not only showed gratitude but memory too. That 'gator knew me as soon as he saw me. He saw I was in trouble and knowed a way to keep me out. He did it, and thus showed his grat-itude."

"Didn't you feel ticklish walking over that living bridge?" inquired the major.

"I did at first," was the reply, "but the big 'gator walked over with me, and he kept up a low sort of growling that seemed to skeer the others and they kept as still as mice."

"I wonder what the judge had been drinking that day," said the professor, sotto voce.

"That 'gator always seemed as if he couldn't do enough for me," continued the judge. "One day I was sitting on the bank, and he had crawled close up where he could look at me. A sudden storm came up and the sky was full of lightning. One big flash came right at me, but the 'gator was quicker than it and jumped right in front of me. It didn't seem to phaze him one bit, and I wondered where it had gone to. Imagine my surprise when he opened his mouth and spit out about six feet of the prettiest lightning I ever saw in my life."

"Did I ever tell you about learning alligators to play baseball?" said the major.

"No! Well, I believe I won't neither, for I never saw a 'gator play baseball in my life."

"That will do for to-night," said the professor. "Bring on the keerds [cards] and let's go into executive session."

The Gator's Rumble
by E.W. Carswell

E.W. Carswell is a writer, folklorist, former judge, and long-time news-paper man who has lived in Florida's Panhandle since he was born in 1916. He has written sixteen books about that area, including the one from which this excerpt has been taken, He Sold No 'Shine Before Its Time *(Bonifay, FL: Taylor Publications, 1981), compiled and edited by Ray Reynolds. Reprinted with permission of E.W. Carswell.*

I f you've never heard an alligator bellow, you've missed one of the world's great animal sounds. It is a rhythmic rumble rather than a bull-like bellow.

As a little boy, I often heard their voices coming from a huge lake near my home. The terrifying voice of what I assumed to be a bull alligator rumbled above the clamor of perhaps millions of frogs, as if to announce that "I'm king of this lake and its environs." Others sometimes responded in a ponderous, pulsing chorus, as if to empha-size the royal announcement. Or so I imagined.

The rumbling, vibrating chorus seemed to shake the swampy earth around the lake, disturbing the water birds and causing trees to tremble. Those voices of doom sometimes scared me a little, too, and I noticed that our cattle accepted the rumble as a signal to seek higher ground.

There was something fascinating about the roar of a big alligator, rolling like low-keyed thunder from the dark waters of the lake. It was an ancient sound, one echoing the age of the reptiles, when cold-blooded creatures ruled the earth.

As I gradually lost some of my fear, I often ventured to the water's edge, hoping to get a glimpse of the great reptiles. I could seldom see them, but I always felt that they were quietly eyeing me from some semi-submerged vantage point nearby. That feeling was intensified by the presence of their tracks on the apron of sand that formed a small beach at the edge of the lake.

The heavy bird-like tracks, often bigger than my hand, told me the size of the alligator. The distance of the tracks apart, and the size of the saurian's tail imprint in the sand, told me more.

I was soon to learn that alligators are not without the instincts and perhaps emotions of many other animals. The rumbling bellow, for example, is actually a tender love call. Alligator courtship includes a lot of dashing, circling and splashing, somewhat in the manner of other creatures. The female is an egg-layer, of course, and she guards her nest with zealousness unknown to egg-layers of the barnyard variety.

It has been a long time since I've heard that once-familiar low-key call in springtime, signifying that a neighboring alligator's fancies had turned to love. But it is a call that I now know to be one of the oldest animal sounds of this earth. And it is one that I'm sure I'll never forget.

The Legend of Two-Toed Tom
by E.W. Carswell

This second story by Judge Carswell takes place in Holmes County, a Florida county east of Pensacola and west of Tallahassee. Beginning in the 1980s, Esto, a small Florida Panhandle town mentioned in this story, held the Two-Toed Tom Festival, featuring food, entertainment, and storytelling about the giant gator. Interest in this particular gator, affectionately called "Triple T," grew with the publication of Carswell's history of the area and the book from which the following story is excerpted, Homesteading *(Chipley, FL: E.W. Carswell, 1986, pp. 135-38), edited by Ray Reynolds. Reprinted with permission of E.W. Carswell.*

The gator, or saurian, in this story supposedly lost three of his toes from his left front paw to a steel trap. Like mythical creatures elsewhere, Old Triple T seems to have been blamed for many area misdeeds that he probably had nothing to do with.

The legend of Two-Toed Tom, the perhaps mythical alligator that terrorized South Alabama a half century ago, lives on in Holmes County folklore, especially in the northern portion of the county near Esto and Noma. Even now, according to a growing version of the legend, he may be living in quiet comfort in the environs of Boynton Island near the forks of Holmes Creek and the Choctawhatchee River.

It is in some of the dark holes of what's known as the Old River that Old Tom may be lurking. He's referred to in the area as Old Tom because, if it's really him, he's got to be old. He was old even when he gained enduring fame in Carl Carmer's book, *Stars Fell on Alabama*. That was many decades ago. When last seen, according to Carmer's account, Old Tom was headed for Florida. Some tracks resembling his have been seen on the western shore of Boynton Island not far from the entrance to a stream called the Little Cutoff.

He gained the name Two-Toed Tom from his track, which showed only two toes on one foot. Old Tom was credited with just about every kind of high crime imaginable, including eating mules and children and attacking women. Old Tom had the uncanny ability, according to the

Going back where he belongs.
Credit: Florida State Archives

Coming out of the lake for a look-see.
Credit: Florida State Archives

story, of escaping the noose of groups bent on his destruction. They would be hunting for him in some likely place near the scene of one of his alleged forays, and he'd be reported miles away. He got credited with much that he didn't do and may not have been guilty of any wrongdoing. But he gained such a reputation that when something bad happened, that terrible Two-Toed Tom got the blame. That two-toed track, whether actually seen or imagined, would be introduced as circumstantial evidence.

No one, it seems, actually saw Two-Toed Tom do all these dastardly things. It was the presence of the tell-tale tracks that convicted him in the public mind. Residents of one South Alabama community thought they'd get him for sure by dynamiting a pond near the scene of one of his alleged crimes. They blasted the daylights out of the pond, along with some neighboring ponds, but Old Tom was up to his old tricks. The dynamiters soon learned that he was miles away stirring up hysteria in another community. The Alabama people undoubtedly breathed easier when they heard he had crossed over into Florida.

Old Two-Toe didn't go far into Florida, however, at least not for a while, if subsequent reports have much substance. It was not long until someone reported getting a fleeting glimpse of an unbelievably big alligator in Sand Hammock Lake, in northern Holmes County. But like the Loch Ness Monster, he quickly vanished from view. Someone reported that the mammoth reptile left an ominous two-toed track on the sand near the southern end of the lake. Few people in the neighborhood at the time doubted that Old Two-Toe was actually there. He was an enormously big bull gator, being "big papa" in that 80-acre lake. He was reported to have a harem.

Early each morning in late spring and early summer, Old Two-Toe (if that's who it was) would begin bellowing, usually at the northern end of the lake. If you've never heard a really big bull gator bellow, then you've missed one of life's memorable experiences. It was a deep-throated rumble that easily could be mistaken for the voice of doom. It could be heard for great distances, maybe for miles, disturbing cattle, scaring mules and horses, frightening chickens and sheep and prompting mothers to warn their children not to stray far from home. Actually, that warning wasn't necessary. Few children dared stray far, not with Old Tom sounding off in the neighborhood.

Old Tom loved to start bellowing at one end of the lake and then move slowly to the opposite end and back. By then, every living creature within or anywhere near the lake acknowledged that it was his turf. Waters of the lake quivered and the ground trembled in the lowlands around the lake from the sound of his deep bass voice. He was a big rascal, all right. Some teen-age boys in the neighborhood reported getting a glimpse of him now and then. They swore he was at least 18 feet long, maybe even up to 24 feet. Some of them reported seeing his tracks in the sand beside the lake, but something always seemed to happen to abolish the evidence.

One of the boys swore he got close enough to tell that the big reptile was a "red-eyed gator." Everyone in the neighborhood knew that "red-eyed gators" were the worst kind. Some of the bigger boys said they'd fired at the big alligator time and again with .22 caliber rifles and with shotguns. But they swore that the bullets and buckshot pellets shattered off the gator's thick hide much as dry peas would after being tossed onto a tin roof.

A long drought descended on the region as that summer wore on, and soon Old Two-Toe's voice could be heard no more. Some nearby residents, talking knowingly of such things, said it signalled the end of the mating season. Others, declaring that Old Two-Toe was a philanderer of the worst sort, guessed that he simply had grown tired of the female companionship in the Old Sand Hammock and had gone on the prowl. They could have been right, because some of the other gators also left. Their tracks could be seen heading south. At least one of the bigger ones went in that direction, walking down a dirt road as if he owned the right of way.

He was unobserved for more than a fourth of a mile, and he might not have been noticed then if it hadn't been for Mrs. Jay Toole and her little daughter, Mary. Mrs. Toole and Mary, who was only about four years old, had crossed the road from their home to a vegetable garden on the other side. They were returning, with little Mary tagging along maybe 40 or 50 steps behind her mother, when some motherly intuition prompted Mrs. Toole to look back.

There across the road was little Mary, all right, but the big gator had walked between the two. Mrs. Toole screamed. But little Mary, who apparently hadn't heard about Old Tom and his kin, kept trying to cross to her mother despite the presence in the road of the strange creature. The gator raised tall on his four feet and hissed a horrible hiss at Mrs. Toole, who kept his attention with her screaming and bare-handed threatening until he finally moved aside enough for the mother to reach her daughter.

By that time neighbors began gathering. Some soon brought shotguns and .22s. But they found that they couldn't do much damage with such weapons. Harmon Holland finally came from a half mile away with his Springfield or Winchester, commonly called a "war rifle" by the boys in the neighborhood. All he needed to get someone with that rifle was an address, according to rumors that had spread among the boys. But it took more than one shot to get that gator. It took several to bash in his head and make him call it quits.

The gator was hitched behind a farm wagon and dragged like a log off into the woods to be left for the buzzards. Distant neighbors kept coming to view the remains. One of them decided to cut himself off a hunk of gator tail steak, but he changed his mind suddenly when that "dead" gator knocked him a-winding with his powerful tail.

Just about everyone at first thought the gator was the legendary Two-Toe. They did, that is, until they got a chance to look at his feet. Each had a full set of toes. It was then assumed that the dead gator was maybe the biggest of Old Two-Toe's sons. He was somewhat less than 14 feet long, far too short to be Old Two-Toe himself. After all, wasn't it assumed that Two-Toe had gone? No one had heard him bellow for

Alligator eggs for breakfast, 1910s.
Credit: Florida State Archives

days. And they never did again, not around the Old Sand Hammock. He may even then have been working his way southward into the remote recesses of the Choctawhatchee-Holmes Creek swamp.

Maybe he had been seeking to escape the dangers posed by people who kept trying to blame him for things he didn't do, and trying to shoot him. Or maybe he was just romantically inclined and was out seeking greener pastures. Pastures don't come any greener, perhaps from a gator's point of view, than Boynton Island and environs. Maybe he has lived there undetected all these years dining off of nature's bounty. If he catches a wild hog or a deer now and then, no one pays much attention. The mule population has declined drastically in the area, but no one apparently has blamed alligators.

It is probable that no one would have suspected his continued presence had not the river reached a record low-level during a drought. This made it necessary for an unbelievably big alligator to walk across a sand bar to climb a gooey mud bank to get onto the island. In doing so, he left some tremendous tracks. He had a little trouble climbing up that mud-coated embankment. It wasn't clear that he succeeded, but he did leave a clear imprint of his feet, including one that had only two toes.

Efforts in the meantime to catch a glimpse of the big saurian have been futile. He or some other big gator surfaces now and then at scattered places around the island, but no one has had a chance for a truly good look. Like the Loch Ness Monster, he seems to vanish after giving an occasional onlooker a flirting glimpse. And his voice, which he doesn't exercise often, is said to be a ghostly reminder or a hoarse whisper of an ancient river steamer with a half-head of steam.

If it is indeed Old Two-Toe, and no one in the neighborhood is saying for sure it is, then he has aged about 60 years in the meantime. Such a crafty creature can gain a lot of wisdom in 60 years. He already must have been hundreds of years old, according to the legend that followed him from South Alabama. Such a cunning creature can get mighty mean in that length of time, too. But actually he may have mellowed with age. He seems at least to be minding his own business, be he Old Two-Toe or some other gator.

Algy the Alligator
by E.C. Bradford

This story comes from a collection of fiction by writers who were members of the Writers' Workshops at Cornell University. One word in the story that might need explaining is smelt, as in "Deader'n a smelt." The word refers to a dead fish or to something melted down in a furnace. The story appeared in Writers For Tomorrow *(Ithaca, NY: Cornell University Press, 1948, pp. 84–90), edited by Baxter Hathaway. Reprinted with permission of the publisher.*

O ver by the window several men gazed down, the equal angles of their bowed heads producing an almost reverential appearance. The object of their attention was a motionless, dirty alligator about six feet long, half-submerged in a water tank not much bigger than the beast itself. A noticeable, but not overpowering, musky odor permeated the entire bar.

"Hey Mac! Give us break, will ya? How about a couple of beers down here?"

Mac, solidly bay-windowed, with white shirt and apron, stood slightly apart, gazing out at the people passing under the street lights. The thirsty one turned to his partner.

"A man can't even get an honest beer here anymore on account of that damn animal."

"That's for sure. Mac's turned into one of the zoo-ologists since he got the damn thing. All he does is stand over there and argue with the first guy that comes along."

Mac ignored them as he put down the beers, so the two men nodded sagely and returned to the contemplation of their glasses. A slight gust of fresh, cool air indicated the arrival of a new customer who spotted the small group of men near him and went over quietly to discover what the center of interest was.

"Why it's a goddam crocodile!" he shouted, and looked around for someone to explain its presence. A hushed, expectant silence fell on the room, and all eyes turned to view the perpetrator of this sacrilege.

"That's an alli—why hello, George!" shouted Mac. "When did you get out? C'mon. Let's have a drink."

They went back to the bar together, and the noise resumed, customers disappointed by the sudden collapse of a good argument. "You're lookin' good, George. Navy must have shaped you up. Where did you get sprung?"

"Up at the Lakes a few days ago. Where in hell did you get that animal, Mac? God, how it stinks!"

"A guy sent it to me. He must have been drunk when he did it. Good for business, though."

George laughed. "Yeah. I'll bet. He's probably dead, and you don't know it." He took a drink and shook his head, smiling.

"Naw. That's just the water. And furthermore, henceforth, kindly refer to him as Algernon. Algy for short."

"Aye, aye, sir!" George snapped to attention and thumbed his nose.

"That's better. Now stick around, why dontcha, and help me close up."

Hours later, the streets were empty, and the neon signs were out, and a few bare night lights shone from the inner recesses of several stores. Closer inspection showed one of these, a bar, still inhabited by two men. They were Mac and George, hanging over the edge of the tank, drinks in hand. Mac had checked out the night's take, and they were having a few after-hours' drinks in memory of old times. George was talking.

"And d'you know where you'd be, Mac, if that male alligator didn't eat those nine hundred and ninety-nine thousand nine hundred and ninety-nine alligator eggs? Do you?"

"No, I don't know. And furthermore, George, I don't give a damn."

There was a moment's silence while George slowly shook his head in despair.

"Well, Mac, you'd be up to your neck in alligator eggs. That's where you'd be."

Mac stood up straight, slowly assuming all his drunk dignity.

"George, do you mean to stand there, takin' half an hour to tell that damn story, and end up with a punch line like that? Jesus!" He leaned over and spat decisively into the tank. "Why, it's an insult to Algy down there."

"You just ain't got any sense of humor, Mac. That's your trouble." He paused. "And furthermore, that damn alligator or crocodile or whatever it is, is dead, stinks, and you ought to get rid of it."

An early alligator zoo.
Credit: Florida State Archives

"Dead my eye! He's hibernatin'!"

"Hibernatin'! That's sump'n bears do in the winter time when they get cold. Whoever heard of a hibernatin' alligator?"

"They do, dammit! They climb in a mud bath like some of these high society women and wait for water!"

They sipped their drinks in silence for a few minutes, staring out the window into the darkness, watching a few lone figures pass under the street light. George spoke slowly.

"Mac. There ain't no mud. He's got water. It's warm in here. I tell you the damn thing's dead. Why don't you get a stick and poke him and see?"

"Oh, all right. But don't blame me if you get soakin' wet when he starts bangin' around."

Mac walked off toward the back, pushing off each chair as it came along. He stayed in the dark outside the bald glare of the old desk lamp, used for a night light. There was a new cop on the beat. After a while he returned, carrying an old broom over his shoulder, mumbling "Hut two, hut two," to himself. When he came up to the tank, he tried to click his heels and nearly fell in. George watched him with a condescending smile.

"You're showing your age, Mac."

"Where?" He twisted around as a woman might, looking for a recalcitrant slip.

"Give me the goddamn broom and quit clowning." George grabbed it out of his hands and aimed the handle at Algy's snout. The first stroke was a light one, with no results. The second time, he gave it a resounding crack, and the head ducked a little and came up. The veiled eyes were motionless.

"You see, Mac? What'd I tell you?" He shifted the broom and started poking away at Algy's side. The rocking body splashed water on the sides of the tank and then was still.

"Deader'n a smelt, and that's all there is to it."

"Dammit, George. I can't believe it. Sorta liked the old bird. Here. Gimme the broom." He belabored the beast until beads of sweat were running off his nose, and still nothing happened. "Well, let's have another and think it over." They moved over to the bar.

"What the hell are we goin' to do with it?"

"'We!' It's your alligator, not mine. Wait until he starts really stinkin'. This whole block'll be deserted." George chuckled softly to himself and sipped his drink. "Yessir, Mac, you mix a mean drink. If it weren't for Algy there you'd have a good business, but as it is—" A slow shake of his head made his point. His expression changed to one of deep thought. Silence reigned.

"Well, Mac. We could put it out with the garbage."

"Yeah. S'pose we could. Think of the poor garbage man's feelings though. Might shock him. Might have a bad ticker."

"Yeah. Pity the poor garbage man."

They looked down at their drinks, thinking of the poor garbage man when he saw Algy. Poor dead Algy. Poor garbage man. They shook their heads in unison. Then George spoke again. He was full of ideas.

"Chuck him in the river. That'd do it. That's the answer."

"Hey! Could be you got somethin' there, George." He thought a moment. "Nope. Won't work. He'd probably float and scare everybody for twenty miles down the river. And then when that City Sanitary Department or whatever it is heard about it, they'd be down here in no time. Everybody knows about him. Hell, he even got a write-up in the Chronicle. I'd lose my license."

"Yeah. Guess you're right, Mac." More silence.

"How about a cigarette?"

"Sure. Thanks."

George struck a match and lighted them, then slowly watched the flame creep down to his fingers. He dropped it quickly and shook his hand. The heat always seemed to beat the flame.

"By God, that's what we'll do!"

"Do what?"

"Why, Mac, it's a cinch. We'll burn the damn thing. You know, cremate him."

"How'll we do that? Where would we do it? It'd sure look funny, burning up an alligator on the sidewalk."

"No, no, Mac. In the furnace! See? In the furnace."

Mac was silent for a moment. He conjured up the furnace in his mind, comparing sizes. It seemed too simple somehow.

"Well, I guess we could, at that. It'll be a helluva job gettin' him down there though."

"Easier than draggin' him all over town."

"Well, let's get started then. It's gettin' late."

They got up and went over to look in the tank again.

"How much d'you suppose he weighs, Mac?"

"Dunno. Two or three hundred pounds, I guess. Heavier'n hell anyway."

"Guess we'll have to get right in there with him then. Roll up your pants and let's go."

They both laboriously climbed into the tank. Mac slipped and almost fell. The water felt awful cold. George leaned over and grabbed Algy under the forelegs, and Mac, grunting and cursing, got a good grip just forward of the hind legs. He had a harder job because the tail was in his way.

"Okay, Mac. One, two, three, heave!"

Algy came up a lot easier than they expected, and they had to drop him with a crash on the floor in order to catch their balance.

"Boy! If that didn't wake him, nothin' will."

They splashed out of the tank and walked around to look at him closely. A stale, putrid smell arose from the tank, the mighty struggle having stirred up the muck on the bottom.

"Here we go again," said George, and they slowly lifted him up, staggering under the weight. Water dripped slowly off of the tip of Algy's tail, leaving a wet trail as they weaved back and forth, tacking for the cellar door.

"Wait a minute, George!" shouted Mac, but it was too late. In the dark, George missed his footing and fell headlong.

Mac just let go everything and stood at the top of the stairs. The reverberations of an ash can finally settled down, and he could hear a string of consummate profanity rising from the depths. He switched on the light but couldn't see a thing through the heavy cloud of dust.

"You all right, George?"

"Hell yes! C'mere and get this goddam thing off me. My God what a stink!"

Mac clattered down the stairs, and through the haze he could see George flat on his back, almost completely covered by the alligator. Both were a sort of uniform gray color from the ashes. Mac grabbed the tail and hauled Algy off poor George, who got up slowly, cursing, feeling himself all over for hidden wounds.

"You're sure you're all right, George?"

"Goddammit, Mac, yes! I do that sort of thing every day. Now open that damn door, and let's shove him in. I'm sick and tired of the whole business."

Mac was silent. He didn't want to lose his friend's help at this late date. He went over and opened up the furnace door and looked in. Good fire. He opened the bottom door to increase the draft and then walked over to his post at the rear of Algy. This time they worked silently and swiftly. George shoved his end in and helped push from the rear with Mac. They could hear water sizzling on the coals. Part of the tail still stuck out, but they wrestled it in and slammed the door.

"There, bigod." George was slapping his hands trying to get the dirt off. "Now let's wash up and have a drink." He started for the stairs.

"Wait a minute, George! Listen!"

They could hear a slow movement inside the furnace, and then all hell broke loose. The din was so loud that George and Mac couldn't hear each other. Bang! Bang! Bang! The rusty old side plates of the furnace were flaking off rust. Rivets were popping, cinders flying.

"Shall we let him out?" Mac yelled.

"Hell no! He'll eat us alive. Let's get out of here. Holy Moses, what a racket!"

They both tore up the stairs and slammed the door, deadening the uproar a little bit. Mac poured a couple of stiff ones with shaking hand, and they stood there, looking into the bar mirror, listening to the noise below. It slowly died down and they started breathing easier.

"Think it hurt him much, George?"

"Naw. Probably suffocated before he burned much."

They sipped their drinks silently, not daring to look at each other.

"My God, George, look!"

George looked. "Judas Priest!"

They both rushed for the cellar door where smoke was seeping out around the cracks. Mac got there first and tore the door open. Great billows of smoke almost knocked him down, so he slammed the door shut again and ran to the phone.

"Operator! Operator! There's a fire up here on the corner of White and Boyle! Yeah! 'Ye Olde Taverne.' Get 'em up here quick!"

He slammed down the receiver and turned to look at George. George merely shrugged his shoulders. He'd had enough. Nothing would ever bother him again. They went to the street door and opened it wide. Mac flicked on the lights, as they heard the sirens wailing and bells clanging. The trucks screeched to a stop, and men piled off, dragging the hose to the hydrant. They hooked it up swiftly and roared through the bar with the hose, tipping over the tables and chairs. The nozzle man whipped open the cellar door and plunged into the smoke as it billowed out into the bar.

It didn't last long. There were a few shouts and curses and the sound of rushing water under high pressure. Then they started banging up the stairs again.

"Well, fella," said one begrimed individual to Mac, "the fire's out, but there's one damn mad crocodile or alligator or something down there. Don't know what you're going to do with him. He's bitter."

II. Other Animals Versus Gators

When we think of a fight between an alligator and another animal, we usually think that the gator will win. But that's not always the case.

Crocodile vs. 'Gator

The following story was printed in The Miami Metropolis *(Miami, Florida, July 30, 1897, p. 1). Among the terms to be explained in this story are* Conchs—*people who live in the Florida Keys and who like to eat the marine mollusks found there;* wreckers—*those who made a living salvaging wrecked ships, especially in the Florida Keys;* fruiter—*a ship that carries fruit; and* Nile god—*the crocodile. Although the author equates "Conchs" and "wreckers," the two were not necessarily the same. Many Conchs were wreckers, but not all of them were.*

THE FIERCE BATTLE TOOK PLACE AT CARDS SOUND
HUNDREDS OF EXCITED PEOPLE WERE PRESENT
THE CONCHS BACKED THE CROCODILE VERY HEAVILY, BUT THE 'GATOR WON THE VICTORY AFTER TEARING HIS ANTAGONIST TO PIECES

Ask N.S. Shaylor, professor of geology at Harvard, if there are any crocodiles in the State of Florida and he will tell you yes. He was sent to Florida a year or so ago to make an investigation as to how far the coral formation extended into the Everglades, and while at Cards Sound, in the lower end of Biscayne Bay, he saw a crocodile that measured 18 feet from tip to tip. The "Conchs," or wreckers, who live on the coral keys among the ten thousand islands that stretch from Biscayne Bay to Key West, are quite familiar with the reptiles and claim to have seen them 25 feet long.

The crocodile and the alligator both inhabit the waters of Florida, but only in Okeechobee are they found together, and there the crocodiles are scarce and the alligators exceedingly numerous. This fact indicates that the alligators are the greatest warriors, but the fact was never demonstrated until recently, when a 15-foot 'gator and a crocodile six inches longer were pitted in the ring together.

Captain John Gibbs, of the little fruiter Fleetwing which plies among the keys, was in Jacksonville the other day and gave a vivid description of the battle, which attracted so much attention that the

A crocodile has a more pointed snout than an alligator.
Credit: Florida State Archives

wreckers flocked to Cards Sound in their sloops from a radius of fifty miles to witness it.

Tom Jackson and his crowd, from Lower Matecumbe Key, had ensnared the crocodile and with great difficulty had brought him to Cards Sound, where they put him in a big tank surrounded by a wire fence and issued a challenge to pit him against any 'gator in the universe for anything from 100 pounds of sponge to a full-rigged wrecker. Joe Frazee, who is known as "Alligator Joe" among many of the sportsmen who visit Palm Beach and Miami, heard of the challenge and procured the 'gator, accepted and got backing for $200. His pet was penned alongside the crocodile, a partition being between. The fight was set for July 5 and the news spread so fast that soon two factions were formed, one backing the 'gator and the other the Nile god. When the thin partition was torn from between the two pens, there must have been 500 men and boys on hand to see the fun.

THE STRUGGLE BEGINS

It was then that the points of difference between the two beasts might be observed. The 'gator was much broader than the crocodile, but did not have the same length of jaw or such immense teeth as his antagonist. He seemed to be stronger in the body, but looked blacker and more sluggish, except in turning, when he was much quicker. The crocodile, on the other hand, was long, sinuous, a tanned leather color, and his tusks actually protruded through his upper jaw. Captain Gibbs says that the articulation of the jaws was the greatest point of difference. The upper jaw of the alligator was immovable, while that of the crocodile was exactly the opposite.

They were unleashed, the crowd cheering. The alligator, as soon as he saw his old foe, lifted his great lumbering body off the earth and literally trotted toward him, roaring horribly the while. The crocodile roared back like an angry bull and prepared himself for the onslaught.

Five feet away the alligator paused, eyed the crocodile like a pugilist eyes his opponent, shifted a bit to one side, opened wide his jaws, found jaws opened even wider to meet him, backed off a step or two, moved forward again, circled around, wheeled and struck the crocodile a blow with his tail that would have killed a mule. The noise sounded like the rending of a sail in a gale, and the force of it knocked the pet of the "Conchs" over and over. It was clearly the first knock-down.

FRANTIC WITH DELIGHT

The Frazee crowd were frantic with delight and offered two to one on their champion, with ready takers.

The alligator lost no time in seizing his advantage, but the crocodile was as quick in regaining his feet and sailed in to get a jaw-hold. Both got one, rose up in the air together like wrestlers and parted, the alligator rending an immense piece of flesh and hide out of his antagonist's neck, but losing a whole foreleg, the bones of which had been ground to a pulp in the crocodile's jaw.

From then on they wasted no time in sparring for wind, but clashed together, rose up in the air and parted, sometimes with a nip and sometimes with a whole mouthful of flesh and blood.

These gators don't want to fight anyone or anything.
Credit: Florida State Archives

In one of the rallies the crocodile got the 'gator amidships and tore out yards of entrail, leaving a great hole in the saurian's side. But what would have daunted a pugilist and have caused his seconds to run wildly for a physician was nothing to the 'gator, who fought on with redoubled fury, getting as his share in that bout about three feet of his antagonist's tail, nailing him tremendous blows with his great flail at every opportunity, the crocodile responding with the same kind of blows, lacking it seemed, however, in brute strength.

JAWS LOCKED

Finally, after the excitement was at fever heat, and when the betting was even money on each reptile, they clashed together, got their jaws locked, jaw in jaw, and rolled over and over like bulldogs, never letting go until something broke and came. It was in this round that the anatomy of the alligator proved him the superior beast. The crocodile had him by the upper jaw, the alligator had the crocodile by the lower jaw, and the lower jaw of that beast was broken into fragments of ivory and bone. The fight was practically over, but there was a finish to it, and in the finish the crocodile never turned tail, but remained in the ring and fought until he was literally torn to pieces.

The Jackson boys were greatly chagrined and sailed home in their boats, hundreds of pounds of sponges and a dozen or two sloops the losers.

A Shark Attacks an Alligator

This story, which appeared in The Palatka Daily News *(Palatka, Florida, May 14, 1884, p. 1), describes a deadly encounter between a shark and an alligator, with results that may surprise readers.*

On last Friday, a combat between a ten-foot man-eater shark and a seven-foot alligator was witnessed at East Pass, near Pilot Cove. When his sharkship spied the alligator, he went for him at a lively rate, cleaving the water with incredible rapidity. The alligator stood his ground and waited the onslaught with blinking eyes and open mouth. Seeing his antagonist prepared for him, the wily shark made only a seeming attempt at attack and rushed by his gatorship with increased velocity. When a few feet only intervened, the shark, by a turn known only to this fish, wheeled with lightning rapidity and pounced upon his enemy. Quick as the movement was, it did not succeed. As the saurian and the fish came together, there was a terrible churning of the phosphorescent waters for a moment, and then the shark darted off a few feet, turned once more quickly upon its stomach, and his ponderous jaws closed upon the saurian's middle. Then there was a crushing of bones and flesh for a second, the water was dyed with the saurian's life blood, and then one-half of the defeated foe was seen to disappear down the cavernous throat of the shark.

An Elephant and Two Camels Attacked by Alligators

This horrific story, which was published in the Tallahassee Sentinel *(Tallahassee, Florida, February 19, 1870, p. 1), describes how a vicious pack of alligators attacked some circus animals.*

AN ELEPHANT AND TWO CAMELS ATTACKED BY ALLIGATORS IN A FLORIDA SWAMP. TERRIFIC BATTLE, AND DEATH OF ONE CAMEL, TWO DOGS AND A COLT

T he peregrinations of showmen are beset with numerous difficulties while pursuing their daily avocations in this, our Southern country, which with the usual winter rains, heavy roads, and fording of streams, makes it very difficult for the managers to make good the promises of the agents. Such was the case with John Robinson's Circus and Menagerie a few days since. While performing in Tallahassee, Fla., it was mentioned to Mr. J.F. Robinson, Jr., that he might expect some difficulty in passing through a long and dismal swamp between that place and Quincy on account of the large number of alligators which infested the ford at this particular locality and who are, at this season of the year, very ferocious and on the watch for any unfortunate mule or horse that may become entangled in the numerous roots, quicksands, and holes which abound at the ford, but he replied, as the agent had already made the arrangements for him to go through and it was not his nature to turn back he had nothing left but to follow, trusting in his future good fortune in getting thus far. The result of decision, although anticipating some difficulty, was far more serious than he anticipated.

At three o'clock p.m. on Tuesday, January 25th, Prof. Lindy Houston, who has charge of the animals, started with the elephant empress, the large Bactrian camel, the beautiful Arabian white camel, a fine thoroughbred mare and colt, and two spotted coach dogs to make the trip to Quincy, although repeatedly warned by Mr. J.F. Robinson, Jr. not to attempt the passage of the swamp in any other than daylight. He

An alligator can seem quite docile, especially when you're
*sitting on him. **Credit: Florida State Archives***

however went through. Before approaching the ford, an occasional bellow or roar was heard betokening that the inhabitants of the locality had not retired for the night, and a sudden plunge and splash in the water would denote that the enemy were on the alert for mischief. The elephant would, every few steps, throw her trunk aloft, emitting at the same time a loud screech of defiance, the camels uttering low moanings, while the horses refused to stir, and stood trembling with fear, while the dogs kept up an incessant howling. Approaching the water of the ford, Houston determined upon the immediate passage through before the alligators had time to summon their crew.

Bidding the elephant enter, she stepped boldly in, at the same time lashing the water furiously with her trunk, the camels, horses and dogs following close in the rear. He had passed two-thirds of the way, when a sharp yelp of pain from one of the dogs and his sudden disappearance denoted that the swamp fiends were at work, and before he could collect his thoughts the other dog went under with a long death howl. He now began to think of his own safety, and calling to the elephant, commanded to her to turn, as she did. So a fearful roar was heard from the large Bactrian camel who had at that instant been attacked. The water seemed alive with alligators. The roaring, bellowing and screeching of elephant, camels and alligators were terrific. They would throw their ponderous jaws open and tear huge pieces of flesh from the camel, while the poor brute would utter heartrending groans and cries for relief. In the meantime the elephant was not idle. Ever solicitous for the welfare of her keeper and companions, she had, at the moment of seeing them safely landed upon the opposite shore, rushed back to the assistance of her friend, the camel, who by this time was nearly gone, and by creating the greatest furor among her assailants, succeeded in bringing the head of the camel to the shore, that portion being all that remained of the poor animal.

In the confusion that ensued, Houston did not miss the colt until warned by a shrill scream or neigh, which seemed to come from several rods below. Upon rushing down the stream a few yards a terrible scene was presented to his view. It would seem that the denizens of the Chattachoochee swamp for miles around had become cognizant of some extra attraction at that particular point on this night, and had started for the rendezvous, and upon reaching the scene of action had unexpectedly encountered both food and opposition at the same time, for, simultaneous with the meeting of the colt they met their pursuers, and an awful battle ensued. Several times it seemed as if the colt would escape and regain the shore, so busy were the alligators in destroying each other; but just before the poor creature would reach the land, some monster, more ravenous than brave, would leave the melee, pursue and drag it back into deep water, until finally it became exhausted and fell an easy prey to the fearful reptiles, while Professor Houston stood looking on with blanched and terrified looks, wholly unable to render the least assistance, threatened with terrible death should he even attempt it. As he turned to retrace his steps towards the place where he left the remaining animals, he counted the cost. He had made the passage, but at a terrible sacrifice. He had started with an elephant, two camels, two dogs and two horses. He came out with an elephant, one camel, and one horse. The camel was valued at $5,000 and was very rare. The colt Mr. Robinson had repeatedly refused $1,000 for. It will be many a long year before Houston will forget the horrors of passing through a Florida swamp at night.

Bear and Alligator Fight

This article about a battle between a bear named Bruno and a gator, which appeared in the Tallahassee Sentinel *(Tallahassee, Florida, December 17, 1870, p. 3, slightly altered here), describes a scene that must have astonished those who read it. As with the previous story about a shark and an alligator, the gator faces an animal that can match it in skill and ferocity.*

We learn that a terrible fight took place on one of the upper lakes between a large bear and an alligator. A man was fishing close by the scene of action at the time. When he heard the roar and bellow of both animals, he was disposed to cast away his fishing tackle and run, but finding that the noise of the conflict came no nearer, he cautiously crept through the jungle and there witnessed the combat.

Bruno and his antagonist were in water about eighteen inches deep, the fight was long and severe, and it was terrible, the man said, to see how they lacerated and tore each other. The bear resorting to his peculiar tactics would enfold the alligator in his huge arms, and over and over they rolled in the water until at last the bear came off the victor, leaving his enemy dead, and, as the witness said, came up the bank with much satisfaction shaking himself.

The Lone Bull of Maybank
by Archibald Rutledge

The following story, which appeared in Old Plantation Days *(1900), is another one about an encounter between a bear and an alligator. This one has an unexpected ending.*

Countless white bubbles rose to the surface of the dark swamp water. The lily-pads, anchored by their long black stems, were sliding softly here and there on the surface, moved from the depths of the morass by some invisible power. Gently among the bubbles there then appeared what looked like a walnut, floating on the water. Higher it rose, growing wider, more irregular. Dimly two great eyes in protruding sockets cleared the level of the water. Next, the huge armored body of a bull alligator appeared, monstrous and scaly, looking like a dragon of medieval tapestry. With his body half-submerged and his wicked head thrust partly up on a spongy grass tussock, he lay still in the mellow sunshine, hideously contented.

A gray squirrel, with tail arched divinely, barked at him from a cool retreat among the tender leaves of a sweet-gum. A foolish blue jay, that had been inspecting a pine sapling growing on the edge of the morass, peered impudently at him, scolded him harshly, but suddenly grew afraid, and flew screaming away. The blue and green dragon-flies, that could poise so jauntily on the sere reed tops, whisked daringly over the drowsing alligator, flared in glittering circles above him, and returned with defiant grace to their perches.

Far up in the blue profound of the noonday sky a solitary osprey, which had a nest on the crest of the dead cypress that stood out of the water, gazed down arrogantly on the lord of the morass; for to the enormous old alligator, cruel, cunning and powerful, the community of wild life in that vicinity paid the bitter tribute of a fearful respect. And this realm of the mighty monarch was a kingdom worth ruling.

The lonely morass was on Maybank Plantation, one of the vast rice estates of the old South. For half a century the plantation had been deserted, and nature had long since completed her gracious work of covering the unhappy ruins that showed the trail of man.

For a mile through the pine forest the black channel of the swamp wound a tortuous and sluggish course, having a trickling, weed-choked outlet into the river. On each side of the narrow channel were water-lily beds, marsh tufts, clumps of buck-cypresses and fringes of green and yellow duck oats. Beyond these was a growth of young canes, dense and rustling; and still beyond, the level brown floors of the pine wood swept gently upward and away.

There had been a time when the swamp had swarmed with alligators, when the great bulls had challenged each other from end to end of the dark channel, when the marshbeds held many an armored giant, thawing out the chill of winter in the sweet spring sun. But those days, as the days of the plantation itself, had passed.

Some of the alligators had been killed by wandering negro hunters. During the heat and drought of long summers others had crawled off toward the river in search of fresher water, and had never come back. One by one they had passed, one by one. Only the great bull, the most ancient and powerful of them all, remained.

His deep den under the wide-spreading roots of the osprey-haunted cypress held the source of a spring, so that his water-supply was always fresh. His wariness kept him clear of the few lone hunters who occasionally penetrated those deserted wilds.

As the other alligators left, the problem of his own support became easy for the great alligator. Cruel and slothful was the life that he led. He ruled the swamp, even to its most remote recesses, with a vicious invincible power. Heavy toll he took of the sportive trout that silvered like flashes of sunlight the dark waters of the lagoon; of the gentle and beautiful wood-ducks that built their nests on the low-swinging cypress limbs that brushed the water, trying to rear their fuzzy broods on the retired edges of the tyrant's kingdom; of the tall white egrets, graceful and mild; of the gaunt blue herons that stood in motionless, melancholy ambush, waiting for a chance to pierce or to seize a fish with their javelin beaks; of the wild hogs that rooted on the boggy shores; of the eager hunting-dogs that swam the deep water; of all creatures that came to the haunted morass to drink.

But on this balmy July day, when the monarch with more than usual arrogance viewed his rich domain, moving with indolent strength and assurance among the broad lily-pads, there floated to his nostrils a strange and fascinating odor, musky and penetrating. The nostrils widened until their black pits shone red, the cold, protruding eyes gleamed, and the huge body grew suddenly tense and eager. Determining the direction from which the scent came, the lone bull, almost without a ripple, sank from sight, rising a few seconds later forty yards nearer the shore. Here he lay under some sheltering grass, watching and waiting.

With soft-lunging, padding strides, a brown bear with her little cub, all roly-poly, roguish and playful, came down the pine-scented, flower-bordered wood-path toward the lagoon. The old bear had never been this way before, and she was wary; but the rich beauty and peace of the surrounding swamp, and the gleam of water through the trees, and the cool, delicious aroma of blueberries growing somewhere near made her forget her usual caution and cunning.

The cub, while not equally impressed by the promises of things material, was still equally unsuspicious and perfectly happy. Once or twice when the big bear grunted her affection to him, he answered with a droll squeak of merriment and abandon. He imitated absurdly his mother's rolling gait. To him the whole world was a beautiful play-house, made especially for cubs of his age.

Soon the mother came to a high swamp-blueberry bush, and rearing up, drew the drooping limbs, laden with their misty-purple fruit, eagerly toward her, and crushed the sweet, succulent berries with grunts of satisfied desire.

The cub essayed to follow his mother's example; but the first time he stood up he lost his balance and fell over backward, landing with much amazement but with no injury in a heavy tuft of grass. He rolled over on his side, too lazy for immediate exertion, and gazed with the lambent eyes of indolent admiration at his mother, who was stripping the last branch of its fragrant burden.

The cub swung his feet drowsily back and forth in the air, wondering mildly at his own dexterity. Meanwhile the old bear, with a satisfied rumble, dropped down on her four feet, turned ponderously about, looked at her baby with huge affection, nuzzled him about the sunny grass until he stood up, and then lunged on down the light-and-shade checkered pathway toward the shining water.

Passing a growth of slim cypresses, they came to the rustling cane-brake, like a fringe to the lagoon. The old bear pushed her way through this until her head and shoulders were clear of the canes on the other side. Then she stopped, sniffed the air, and listened. Close behind her, greatly excited because the tips of his furry feet were in the water, the cub palpitated, wondering what this move might mean.

The morass was unknown to the mother, and for that very reason she was apprehensive. But as she listened, she heard nothing to justify her suspicions. The blue sky bent sweetly over them; the gray moss, pendent from every tree, waved silently in the aromatic breeze; two wood-ducks of gorgeous plumage floated peacefully far out on the bosom of the channel. An amiable old bullfrog, seated on a half-submerged mossy tussock, eyed the bears with the air of a kindly patri-arch. A grey sapsucker was following, upside down, the exciting promise of a dead cypress limb.

Still, the mother bear hesitated a long time before she waded into the morass; but some green alligator acorns and some silvery wampee leaves lured her clear of the canebrake. There she began to feed, and there finally she lay down on the quaking turf to wallow. The cub followed manfully, although he kept on a dry ridge of turf that extended out to the channel. He was about ten feet away from his mother. Twenty feet away, with just his eyes and the point of his nose showing above the water, the Maybank bull marked his prey.

The lone alligator was intent on a kill. The musky smell of the bears had stirred his sluggish heart to a dull fever of desire. The tiny brain deep in the monstrous head was aflame with eagerness for blood. His cold, glassy eyes gazed with unwinking speculation at his intended victims. He noticed the old bear's apparent forgetfulness and peace, and the cub's separation from her. Just at that moment the little fellow was trying in vain to make a playmate of a droll stolid terrapin, half-grown, that was trying to pretend that he was really nothing at all.

Measuring the distance and singling the cub as his victim, the alli-gator withdrew silently beneath the black waters. A moment later his eyes rose ever so gently out of the grass-grown lagoon, not six feet from the innocent little bear, which was then slapping playfully at the gaudy dragon-flies as they flirted past him. His mother, although watching him now, was still some distance away, wallowing in the weedy water.

Stealthily, and under the ambush of the glistening wampee leaves, the lone bull drew closer. As he swam softly, he turned so as to give his mighty tail the opportunity to sweep the cub into his crushing jaws. Inch by tragic inch he drew near, leaving but a tiny oily ripple in the water behind him.

There was a short rush, a lunge, the flashing whirl of a mighty tail as of some broad, black scimitar, a terrified squeal from the cub, a furious snort and plunge from the mother. The lone bull's tail had grazed the cub, tumbling him, stunned, into the water; the mother was struggling wildly but vainly in the sucking mud; the red mouth of the great alligator, terrible with tusks, was already open to seize the victim, lying only a foot away.

But then, far from the opposite bank of the lagoon, there came the clear, sharp crack of a rifle, and a white tuft of smoke floated up from the canebrake.

In a moment the scene was vividly changed. The old bear, working free of the morass, had reached the cub and stood defiantly over it, her great sides heaving in the fierce agony of maternal fear. Almost within reach of her paw, turning in slow, blind, painful circles, with a heavy bullet in his brain, was the lone bull of Maybank, helpless, shattered, dying; and his dark blood stained the stagnant waters that he had so long and so cruelly haunted.

Across the lagoon, standing on a fallen log, an old hunter watched this second scene of the tragedy; and even as he watched, the third and last scene was enacted before his eyes. He saw the cub, nuzzled by his fierce old mother, stir feebly; and then the great bear sat back on her haunches, took the cub in her huge, soft arms, rose on her hind legs, and stalked growling out of the morass, disappearing in the purple twilight of the pines.

The hunter could have shot her easily, but being a sportsman and a gentleman, he let the brave old creature carry her baby away in safety. The bull alligator ceased moving, quivered through all his frame, turned slowly over and lay still. And the hunter stepped down from the log and started for his far-off camp.

Then over the great swamp there fell a silence, and such a silence as it had not known in many a year.

For it was a silence that would never be broken by the hollow, terrible roar of the lone bull or the pitiful cries of his victims; but only by the melodious winds choiring through the mighty pines and the songs of happy birds.

III. Humans Versus Gators

Over the past two hundred years, a relatively few brave hearts have made a living by killing alligators, skinning them, and then selling the hides and teeth to others, who make purses, shoes, and other paraphernalia for eager customers.

Kirk Munroe's final sentence in his first essay ("Alligator leather is as popular today as it ever was, and it promises to continue in favor until the last of these uncouth monsters, together with the buffalo of the West and the fur seal of the North, shall have disappeared from the face of the earth.") was a prediction that fortunately did not come to pass. The massive slaughter of alligators in the last half of the nineteenth century and the first half of this century brought the gator to the point of extinction. After state and federal laws were passed to save the alligator from certain extinction, the reptiles have succeeded in recovering and have increased so rapidly that they have become "nuisances" to residents and animals of certain populated areas near lakes. Today, Florida has about a million alligators.

The following stories are about people who hunt gators.

The Alligator Hunters

This newspaper article, which appeared in The Palatka Daily News *(Palatka, Florida, August 24, 1884, p. 3), describes a pair of hunters on their nightly gator hunt. This description can be contrasted with a modern alligator hunt, such as the one that John Moran writes about in Chapter 19.*

LIFE ALONG THE FLORIDA RIVERS IN THE HOT SUMMER MONTHS

The men who hunt alligators for their hides and teeth are reaping their harvest. The warm weather induces great numbers of alligators to frequent the marshy banks of the rivers, and the absence of sportsmen during this season makes them comparatively fearless. The most successful hunters hunt only in dark nights. A few nights ago I had my slumbers broken several times by the discharge of guns. On repairing to the banks of the river the next morning to ascertain the cause of the noise, I found two young men occupying a hastily constructed palmetto fan camp. Six dead alligators were lying around the camp, varying in length from four to eight feet. The hunters had killed them the previous night. One of the young men was busy skinning the alligators, while the other, with the aid of a single cooking utensil, which answered the purpose of baking oven and coffee pot, was preparing a frugal morning meal. The skin is removed from the belly, the under part of the jaws, and the inside of the legs. The skin on the back is worthless. As soon as the skins are removed, they are salted and packed in barrels, which are shipped to a New York firm. The hunters receive $1 apiece for all hides four feet long and upward.

After the skins are removed, the hunters cut off the heads and place them on the edge of the river, where they remain for about a week. At the end of that time, the teeth become so loose that they can be readily pulled out with the fingers. The teeth from half a dozen alligators weigh about a pound, and are worth $4.

The two young men killed fifty alligators in the week that they hunted in this neighborhood. They begin hunting as soon as it becomes thoroughly dark. Their hunting outfit consists of a bull's-eye lantern, in camp language called "look-'em-up," a double-barrelled shotgun or

Alligator hunters in Volusia County, 1913.
Credit: Florida State Archives

"kill-'em-sure," and a hatchet, with which they split the alligator's skull, and to which they have given the very expressive name of "dynamite." The man who is to do the shooting for the night fastens the lantern to his forehead, and takes his place in the bow of the boat. His partner paddles the boat cautiously along the stream, while the man in the bow keeps a sharp lookout for alligator's eyes which under favorable circumstances he can "shine" with his lantern at a distance of two hundred yards. As soon as they discover a pair of eyes, they paddle cautiously up to within a couple of feet of the alligator's head and discharge a load of buckshot into it. As soon as the shot is fired, the paddler catches the alligator by the jaws, which he holds together with one hand, while he cleaves the skull open with his hatchet.

Sometimes the alligators retain considerable power of action. When such is the case, it is rather exciting work getting them into the boat. Sometimes very large alligators turn the boat over. If an alligator is not handled at once after being wounded, he sinks to the bottom and is lost.

I asked one of the hunters, who has killed more than a thousand alligators, what was the size of the largest one he ever killed, and he told me 13½ feet long. He said that his father killed one on the St. Johns River 17½ feet long, the head of which when placed in a flour barrel projected two inches over the top. He sold it to a museum for $65.

Alligator Hunting with Seminoles

by Kirk Munroe

Kirk Munroe (1850–1930) was a popular writer of adventure stories for boys in the late nineteenth and early twentieth centuries. The following story, which is reprinted from Cosmopolitan Magazine *(September 1892), is an account of accompanying Seminoles on an extended hunt for alligators. Terms that may need explaining are* crackers—*people living in isolated, often poor, sections of the state;* sofkee *or* sofky—*hominy or thin corn gruel; and* hardtack—*a hard, crackerlike biscuit.*

In this piece, Munroe writes about the Seminoles in the Everglades: how the Native Americans can quickly build a rain-proof shelter; how they spend long nights on the hunt; and how they use alligator hides as a source of income. The Seminole word allapatta *for "alligator" is the source of the place name* Allapattah *in Miami.*

For hours the long dugout threaded its way, swiftly, and without a pause, through the maze of narrow channels that everywhere intersect the vast swamps of the everglades like a network of veins. These channels are crooked beyond conception, so narrow that we constantly brushed against the tall saw grass forming dense walls on both sides, and so bewildering in their interlacings that one not born and brought up among them would be quickly lost, without hope of extricating his boat from their toils.

The occupants of that particular canoe were Miccochee (little chief), a stalwart young Seminole Indian; Kowika, his twelve-year-old brother; and myself. We had followed one stream up from the coast the day before and were now skirting an edge of the 'glades toward the headwaters of another river on which we proposed to hunt alligators for their hides. That is, my Indian friends were going to hunt alligators, that being their regular and legitimate occupation in life, while I was going to see how they did it, for the benefit of those readers of this magazine to whom alligator hunting is a novelty.

It is seldom that a Seminole can be induced to guide a white man into any part of the everglades, so jealously do the Indians guard the

One way people used to catch alligators.
Credit: Florida State Archives

secrets of this their last place of refuge. Miccochee had not been very enthusiastic over my proposal to accompany him on this trip, but I had once helped Kowika through quite a serious illness, and out of gratitude for this the elder brother finally consented to take me with them. Of course I was greatly delighted at this decision and so was Kowika, for the little chap and I were fast friends.

We travelled in a canoe that Miccochee had fashioned for himself, aided only by fire and hatchet, from a huge cypress log. It was twenty feet long by three broad, and drew about four inches of water. It was propelled by a sail in open waters or through the treeless expanses of the 'glades, and shoved along with a long push-pole through narrow or forest-bordered streams, or when the breeze was unfavorable.

On this occasion we might have sailed; for the limitless sea of brown grasses, stretching to the horizon on every side but one, was level as a floor, and unobstructed by wind breaks; but the breeze, sweeping in salt and strong from the ocean, was dead ahead. The month was March, the thermometer registered 85° in the shade, and the hot sunlight, pouring down from a sky of cloudless blue, glistened on the bare, copper-colored limbs of Miccochee, as, standing with the easy grace of a savage Apollo in the stern of the dugout, he wielded his slender push-pole. He wore but a single garment, a gaudy calico shirt belted about his waist, and his black locks were confined by a crimson handkerchief. Kowika had a bit of cloth fastened about his loins, but was otherwise unadorned. He stood in the bows of the canoe, and fended it off from jutting points with a much lighter pole than that used by his brother. I sat amidships on my blankets; hot, uncomfortable and extremely tired of the monotonous swish of the grasses alongside as well as the steady snapping of the crisp green "bonnet" stems that generally filled the channel.

"How long before we shall make camp?" I inquired of Miccochee at length.

"Bimeby, uncah," was the unsatisfactory response.

"Yes; but when and where?"

"Me fix um, Hin-dle-ote, bimeby." Kowika looked around and grinned.

"But I am getting hungry!"

"Uncah, you like um sofkee? Me like um, bimeby."

That everlasting "bimeby" was as irritating and unsatisfactory as the Cuban "mañana;" but it was Miccochee's word, and would probably have conveyed volumes of information if I had only understood him as well as did Kowika.

A half-hour's silence followed, while the canoe moved swiftly forward. Then from Miccochee came the exclamation of "Hin-dle-ote (good)! Camp now! Bimeby!"

The aspect of our surroundings had changed for the better. We were in a stream that was bearing us forward with a very perceptible current, and our canoe was headed toward the belt of cypress that on that side forms the boundary of the 'glades. In a short time the waving grasses were left behind, and we were gliding through patches of mingled shade and sunlight over dark waters of crystal clearness.

About four o'clock, or "two hour by sun," as the crackers say, the canoe was beached in a little cove that was canopied by the fragrant and widespread tendrils of a huge grapevine. Beyond it a narrow, grassy glade was fringed by the graceful forms of a group of cabbage palms, so that the whole formed one of the most perfect and desirable of camp sites. At one side of it stood a frame of poles and posts, sole relic of some former camp, and before dark Kowika had thatched both roof and sides of this, so as to make a rain-proof shelter, with the great crinkly palmetto leaves that Miccochee and I cut and brought to him. From my own stores I produced coffee, bacon and hardtack. Kowika started a fire and collected wood, and Miccochee speared a couple of fish. They were of a kind unknown to me, but proved of excellent flavor after being wrapped in aromatic leaves and cooked under a bed of glowing coals.

After supper the 200-pound bag of salt that we had brought with us was "toted" into the shanty to keep it from dampness. Then Kowika made beds of the abundant moss that hung in great bunches from the cypresses, while Miccochee and I smoked, and the former overhauled his hunting outfit.

First his rifle, a fine Remington, was carefully examined. Then the harpoon, or "grains" as it is called in that country, was sharpened a bit. It had a keen-edged, two-pronged steel head, loosely fitted to a slender shaft of tough wood, and attached to a coil of small but very strong Manilla line. A fathom of the line nearest the iron was composed of a number of hempen cords that would slip between the teeth of any animal attempting to bite it in two. The item of the outfit that was finally and most carefully examined was a jacklight, to which was attached the crown of an old felt hat, black and greasy with age and long usage.

Until now I had not suspected that all our hunting was to be done at night, but I discovered this to be the case. Darkness had hardly well set in before muttered bellowings began to sound from the stream, both above and below our camp, as well as from the cypress swamp beyond. They were in close imitation of the sounds made by an enraged bull; but I knew that they proceeded from the leathern throats of the very alligators we had come so far to find, for I had learned that lesson some time before. It was given me by a "cracker" with whom I was travelling when I first heard the sound. In my ignorance I remarked that an angry bull was somewhere near us, and expressed surprise, as we were not in a cattle country. At this my companion burst into a loud guffaw, and increased my stock of knowledge by explaining that:

"Them's not bull cows a-bellerin', they's bull 'gators."

On the present occasion Miccochee listened with evident satisfaction to the bellowing for a few minutes, and then remarked:

"Allapatta (alligator) plenty. Me catch um; uncah!"

Lighting the "jack" and fixing the greasy cap, to which it was attached, firmly on his head, he stepped into the canoe and we followed him. The hunter knelt in the bow, grasping his rifle, and the bright jacklight cleaved a gleaming pathway through the inky blackness that now shrouded the river. Beside him, ready to his hand, lay the harpoon, with one end of its coiled line secured to a ringbolt in the sternpiece. I sat amidship, with my rifle across my knees, while Kowika, in the stern, guided the drifting craft with a single-bladed paddle. He dipped it so deftly that not a ripple was created, and we slipped along through the shades of the solemn cypresses without a sound. There were noises enough on every side of us, however. The cries of great herons startled from their roosts by our light, the raucous notes of innumerable frogs, the occasional scream of a panther or snarl of some smaller predatory animal, and above all the deep-voiced bellowing of alligators, gave us plenty to listen to.

I have neglected to mention that during the day we had shot several cormorants, and caught a number of catfish. Just before we started on our nocturnal hunt some of these were tossed into the water, and allowed to float down stream ahead of us, as a bait to attract the alligators.

In noting the weirdness of our surroundings I had almost forgotten the object of the expedition, when it was suddenly recalled with startling distinctness by a blinding flash, a loud report and an exultant yell from Kowika. Alligator number one had ventured out into the stream after a drifting cormorant. He had turned his bewildered gaze toward the approaching light, and, from the darkness beneath it, a rifle ball had crashed into the sluggish brain through one of his glowing eyeballs. The dead body immediately sank, but by feeling along the bottom with his harpoon Miccochee soon found it. A sharp lunge fixed the steel prongs into the scaly side, the shaft was withdrawn with a jerk, and the canoe was headed toward the nearer bank, the coiled line paying out as it went. Two minutes later the dead alligator had been drawn out on a grassy tussock, the harpoon had been cut out, and we were again drifting down with the current.

Within a mile we killed four more of the bewildered monsters, and then turned our prow upstream. Now Miccochee wielded his push-pole from the stern, as only his skill and strength could force the craft in silence against the current. Kowika sat in the middle of the canoe, while I, with jacklight on my head and rifle in hand, occupied the position of honor in the bow.

The only sound as we moved up the stream, keeping close to the bank to avoid the full strength of the current, was the gurgling of water under our bows. The frightened birds had sought other roosting places in the unassailable depths of the swamp, the frogs were silent, and even

A Seminole wrestling a gator in Dania, Florida.
Credit: Florida State Archives

"Open wide!"
Credit: Florida State Archives

the bull alligators had ceased their angry mutterings. I had just arrived at the conclusion that we had either killed or frightened them all, so that none was left, when I was startled by a slight motion on the bank but a few yards away. At the same instant two coals of fire, luridly red, gleamed through the blackness.

What could they be? I was about to speak and direct the hunter's attention to them, when a sharp, warning "hist" from behind conveyed the information, as clearly as words could have done, that my moment for prompt action had arrived. Taking a hasty aim at one of the lurid coals, I fired. The report of the rifle was instantly followed by such a wild rush into the river, such a flurry of whirling, thrashing and splashing, such showers of spray and bloody foam, such a lashing of the water with furious blows and such a commotion generally that it was as if a small but uncommonly vicious cyclone had, without warning, been dropped from the heavens into that quiet spot. Little Kowika screamed shrilly in his excitement; but Miccochee only expressed his displeasure at my bad shot by muttering "Ho-le-wa-gus! Heap bad!"

The flurry lasted but a few minutes, and then the monster sank. "It could not have been such a very bad shot then, for he was dead at last." Thus thinking I laid down my rifle and picked up the harpoon. Feeling cautiously along the bottom I soon brought it in contact with something softer than the rocks, which I prodded with all my strength.

The next instant a huge black form leaped to the surface with a vicious rush, the jacklight disclosed a pair of horrid, wide-open jaws filled with gleaming teeth, there was a bellow like the roar of a wounded lion, and I felt myself being torn and mangled and swallowed and struck by lightning, all at the same instant, that is, I thought I did.

In reality that final effort of the dying monster was only sufficient to bring him to the bows of the canoe, which he struck with such violence as to tumble me over on my face. The thunder-clap that accompanied my involuntary action was the report of my own gun, fired close beside my head, by Kowika. Its muzzle was thrust down the alligator's throat, and before I realized what was happening, he was as dead a 'gator as ever lived, as my friend Dixey Finn would say.

He also proved as large a one as ever lived, in those waters at least, for I measured him as he lay on the bank the next day, and found that he lacked but two inches of being fourteen feet long.

Although I had not covered myself with glory, my alligator had covered me with mud and blood, and drenched me to the skin besides. I had also learned how alligators are hunted by professionals. As this was all I wanted to know just then, and as it was midnight when we again reached camp, I landed and turned in, leaving my Indian friends to continue their hunt as long as they chose.

When I awoke the sun was well up, Miccochee was mending the fire, and Kowika was fast asleep on the opposite side of the shanty. We did not wake him until breakfast was cooked. Then he sat up, completed his toilet by rubbing his eyes, said, "Good how" to me in place of good morning, and was ready for the incidents of the new day.

After breakfast we set forth to view by daylight the result of the night's hunt. To my amazement those two Indians showed me twenty-four dead alligators, drawn up on the river banks within three miles of our camp. They must have continued their hunt until daylight, and could not have had more than an hour or two of sleep when I awoke and found Miccochee already stirring. In spite of this they exhibited no signs of fatigue, but appeared as fresh as when we started on our expedition the day before.

Now began the arduous and to me intensely disagreeable task of skinning the dead 'gators. One of these as we approached him showed signs of life, and Miccochee, reaching across the body, thrust his hunting-knife in to the hilt just behind the fore shoulder on the opposite side. The reason for thus reaching across the body was instantly apparent; for with convulsive energy the mighty tail swept around in that direction with force sufficient to have broken the Indian's legs had he been standing there. It was a final effort, but it might have proved most destructive had not the hunter known just how to deal the death blow.

In watching the operations of skinning I soon discovered that only the underneath, or belly, portion of the hide was to be taken; that the back was too thick and scaly to be worked into leather. As Miccochee explained it:

"Belly, good, hin-dle-ote! Back, hole-wa-gus! White man no like um; no buy um."

Along the sides of each alligator runs a distinct line marking the division between back and belly. On this line, from the end of the snout to tip of the tail, and even around the paws, Kowika made a deep incision with a keen-blade knife, at the same time loosening the skin of the under jaw. Then the carcass was turned over to Miccochee, who, beginning at the head, gradually stripped the skin down the entire length of the body.

Working with the skill of long practice the Indians had those twenty-four alligators skinned and the hides carried to camp by noon.

At the camp they were scraped, and rubbed with a liberal quantity of the salt we had brought with us. Then each was rolled as tightly as possible and stowed away inside the hut, beyond reach of the sun. Early in the afternoon their labors were finished, and they flung themselves on their moss couches for a few hours of sleep before darkness should summon them to resume the hunt.

The atmosphere of the hut was rapidly becoming intolerable to my more sensitive nose; so, while my companions slept, I erected a smaller shanty of poles and thatch at some distance from theirs for my own use. Then I prepared supper, the principal meal of the day on such an expedition, and not until sunset did I arouse the sleepers.

For a week longer the programme of the first night and day was repeated with unvarying regularity, until at the end of that time alligators were scarce in that vicinity, and over a hundred hides, none less than seven feet in length, were stored in the hut. For them the Indians would receive from thirty-five to fifty cents apiece from the trader, upon their delivery at his store, thirty miles away.

By the end of the week I was heartily tired of alligator hunting and impatient to leave that foul-smelling camp. Not only were its immediate odors well-nigh unbearable; but the air for several miles in every direction was laden with the stench arising from the rotting carcasses of the unfortunate alligators. About them, buzzards by the thousand assembled in the daytime, gorging themselves until they could hardly fly; while the night was made hideous by the snarlings and cries of wild-cats and other beasts of prey quarrelling over the loathsome feast. Thus, when the hunt was declared to be ended, I was fully as pleased as I had been a week before at receiving permission to accompany the expedition.

On its return trip our canoe was so deeply laden with its unsavory freight that it was several times necessary, in shoal spots, to unload her, and make a portage to deeper water. At such times, as I "toted" my share of the cargo and reflected upon its ultimate destination, it seemed incredible that these vile skins would soon be transformed into the softest of leather and worked up into the most expensive of travelling bags, belts, card cases, albums and other articles of luxury. But so it is. Alligator leather is as popular today as it ever was, and it promises to continue in favor until the last of these uncouth monsters, together with the buffalo of the West and the fur seal of the North, shall have disappeared from the face of the earth.

Catching Alligators
by Kirk Munroe

This story, reprinted from Harper's Weekly *(April 12, 1884, pp. 233-34), is about the capture of live alligators.*

Although I had gone on many an alligator hunt, of which the object was the killing of these hideous saurians, either for their teeth and hides, or for the purpose of ridding some locality of a pest, I had never assisted in the capturing of one alive, nor had I until very recently any idea of how such captures were effected. Full-grown alligators of from eight to twelve feet in length are common enough in "zoos" and menageries, and in Florida nearly every curiosity shop is provided with a tank in which good-sized specimens are kept and exhibited as advertisements. In regard to these the majority of visitors who have given the subject any consideration whatever have vaguely imagined that they were captured when very young, and allowed to attain their present size in captivity. Some such impression that had lingered in my own mind was thoroughly dispelled one bright January morning as I walked along Bay Street in Jacksonville. Before the doors of one of the many curiosity shops something that excited the lively curiosity of a great crowd of people was being unloaded from a cart. The something proved to be an immense alligator, the largest, as I was afterward told, ever captured alive, measuring thirteen feet four inches from the end of his ugly snout to the tip of his tail, and weighing a trifle over eight hundred pounds.

He was so bound with ropes as to be perfectly helpless, and a gang of stout negroes lifted him from the cart, and carried him to the tank fitted for his reception at the rear of the shop, as they would a great log of wood. In this case the reptile had most evidently not been caught young and brought up by hand, for he bore many marks of a recent violent struggle, and a wiry little old man in torn and muddy clothes, who directed his transfer from cart to tank, was pointed out to me as the captor, and also as the most successful alligator-hunter in Florida. In personal appearance this man was so insignificant that it

Catching live alligators.
Credit: Nineteenth-century **Harper's Weekly**

seemed impossible that any of the stories told of him could be true. He was nearly seventy years of age, so small and spare that his weight could not have been over a hundred and twenty pounds, and he had the sallow, colorless complexion peculiar to the "poor whites," or "crackers," of Florida. Although he had the reputation of being very taciturn upon all matters relating to his business, and the exploits which he regarded in a most matter-of-fact light, upon this occasion he was so elated over the success of this his most notable capture that for once his tongue was loosed, and after the trophy of his skill was safely lodged in its tank, and the crowd had dispersed, I succeeded in drawing from him the following facts:

"Wa'al, mister, long's youm ain't in the business, nor likely to go into it on your own account, I don't mind telling yer how big 'gators is caught. Some fellers makes traps; like ez not you've seen 'em in some of the creeks puttin' in from the St. Johns. They drives a ring of stout stakes in the water, clus to the bank, with an opening to one side. On the side nearest the bank they bends down a sapling with a noose to the end of it, an' jest inside the noose, in the water, they fixes a bait that'll spring the sapling when it's teched. That yanks the 'gator's head up in the yair, an' afore he can git clar they has him bound fast with ropes. That ain't my way, though. Hit's too much work a-fixing of the trap; you has ter wait too long a-watchin' fer the 'gators to come along an' stick ther snouts into it, an' then they'm too all-fired lively with ther tails, when ther heads is cotched, to suit me. Sometimes I fixes a noose on to the end of a spring sapling acrost a runway when it comes handy, an' I've cotched a right smart of 'em that ar way too; but I ginerally goes fer 'em in ther holes, an' digs 'em out.

"You know 'gators allus has holes clus in under the bank. They

A giant caught near DeLand, 1910s.
Credit: Florida State Archives

Alligator Tales

begins in the water; but a leetle back they kinder raises, so's when he's in, he's half outen the water an' half in. Soon's cool weather comes on, 'long in December, theym gits into ther holes an' lies thar quiet like, 'cept on bright warm days, when they come out an' suns. A curus thing is that they allus goes in backwards, an' lies with their noses p'intin' towards the opening. Wa'al, 'long in the fall I watches the 'gators putty clus, an' spots ther runways an' places whar they'm mos' likely to make holes; so by time cool weather sots in I has a dozen or twenty marked. Then when I wants a 'gator I goes fur him an' digs him out.

"How do I manage hit? Why hit's easy 'nuff when you knows how. I usen to take Mandy, my boy, along; but he's got big 'nuff now to go huntin' fer hissef, so I goes alone mos' ginerally. I cotched that thar feller all alone. Not a soul seed him twel I had him tied up an' ready fer market. When I had Mandy along he usen to punch a fence rail into ther hole, an' into ther 'gator's mouth. 'Gator'd grab it, an' hang on like death, an' never let up on his holt long's yer kep' movin' ther rail a leetle. While he was kep' busy an' amoosed like that ar way, I'd dig down into him, an' fust thing he'd know I'd hev a rope round his head an' forepaws. Then I'd dig along back twel I'd git to his hind-paws an' git 'em tied up. But look out fer his tail! When he gits that ar loose, thar's gwine ter be fun, an' mud's gwine ter fly, you bet!

"Yes, sir, this yere feller give me a tussle. Mandy warn't along, an' I tackled him all alone. When I first jabbed the rail down his throat he begun to yank his head this side an' that, twel I 'lowed I was the tail-end of a threshin' machine. But I hung on, an' kep' a-proddin' of him, kase I 'lowed he mought taken it into his head to come outen. When he begun fer to back, I begun fer to dig, an' 'twarn't more than three hours afore I had him dug outen thar, and tied up snug as yer please.

"Yas, 'gators is mighty peart with ther tails; but they can't do nothin' much with their jaws. Them's their weak p'int. Why, sir, I kin cotch that thar 'gator by the end of his jaws with my han's, when hit's mouth's shet, an' hold hit shet spite of all he kin do; but keep outen the way of his tail, fer yer mought jes as well hev a cannon-ball strike yer.

"Does catching 'gators pay? Wa'al, ef a man 'tends to business, he kin make livin' wages at hit. I got twenty-five dollars fer this yere feller, an' prices range 'cordin' to size, so much a foot ginerally, 'bout a dollar to a dollar and a half a foot, fer anything five foot long an' over.

"Little ones? Them I cotches by the hundred in scoop-nets, or digs 'em outen 'long with their mammy. They fotches 'bout a quarter apiece when trade's good. Mos' folkses hain't no idee how to care fer 'em when they gets 'em, an' bimeby they dies outen sheer starvation. You'm got to feed 'em like they was young kittens, and feed 'em in the water. They won't eat nothin' 'less they kin put their heads under water. Feed 'em on bits of raw meat, and put hit right clus to ther noses so's they kin smell hit. They can't find nothin' fer theirselfs ef you throw hit into the water.

"Skins an' teeth? No, ther hain't much doing in them now. Since you Yankee fellers has got to making celluloid teeth and imitation 'gator leather, prices is 'way down; 'bout thirty-five or forty cents is all the hunter gits fer prime hides, nothin' taken less than seven foot long nuther."

Before I left the old hunter he had agreed to send me word when he discovered another exceptionally large alligator, and promised to show me how to "jab" a fence rail down its throat in a manner that would induce him to "hang on an' keep him amoosed."

After keeping the big alligator in a tank for a week or so, and thereby attracting many customers to his shop, the curiosity man sold him to a travelling showman for seventy-five dollars, and Mr. 'Gator is now being exhibited to admiring crowds in the smaller towns of the Southern States.

The curiosity man wishes me to say that he will furnish good healthy alligators, sound in mind and limb, boxed for shipment to any part of the world, and of any size under ten feet long, for two dollars per lineal foot.

Adventures with Alligators

The following anonymous story, which appeared in Harper's Weekly *(January 6, 1883), has two parts: in the first, a gator savagely kills an unsuspecting swimmer, and in the second, two hunters kill many gators, courting danger all the while. Fort Bas(s)inger was established by Colonel (later U.S. President) Zachary Taylor in 1837 during the Second Seminole War and gave the present towns of Fort Basinger and Basinger their names. Some words that may need defining are* hammock—*a low mound of earth prevalent in the Everglades; and* tussock—*a clump of grass.*

L ate one evening last February I sat on the porch of John Pierce's hospitable though modest log house at Fort Bassinger, listening to tales of wild frontier life told by my host and his stalwart sons. Fort Bassinger is situated on the west bank of the Kissimmee River, in South Florida, and is, in that direction, the most advanced outpost of civilization, there being no settlers between it and the dread Okeechobee, fifty miles to the south, and but half a dozen along the whole course of the Kissimmee River, two hundred and fifty miles to the north. It is now a fort only in name, though during the Seminole war it was the site of a permanent encampment of troops. At present Fort Bassinger consists of the log dwelling-house and out-buildings owned by John Pierce, a cattle man, whose wealth lies in the herds which roam the broad prairies of South Florida.

Suddenly, as we talked, the light of a camp fire streamed across the waters of the river a quarter of a mile below the house, and curiosity impelled us to visit the new-comers and inquire concerning them. On reaching the fire we found but one man stretched at length beside it, and patiently watching the roasting of a wild turkey that he had shot some hours before. He was Frank Lefils, the best known and most successful alligator-hunter and guide of South Florida. For nearly twelve years he has made this Floridian wilderness his home, and is intimately acquainted with its most hidden secrets. Clad in hunter's garb, and with hair and beard tawny as a lion's mane, and uncut during his years of sojourn in the wilderness, his personal appearance was as picturesque as it was remarkable.

He was bound for the vicinity of Lake Okeechobee, on an alligator hunt, and readily consented that I should accompany him and share his labors; though he warned me that the trip would be arduous, and not devoid of danger.

We started at daybreak next morning, the hunter in a stanch cypress skiff, and I in the light cedar canoe in which I was exploring those southern wilds. All day long we glided down the swift-flowing crooked river, through its monotonous sameness of wide-spread swamps and lagoons of backwater, "dead rivers," they are called, filled with water-lettuce, bonnets, flags, and the terrible razor-edged sawgrass, but seeing no trace of human occupancy, not even the palm-thatched hut of the wandering Seminole. About five o'clock in the after-noon, or "an hour by sun in the evening," as the crackers express it, we reached a small hammock of cabbage-palms, which we decided to make our camping place and the base of our future operations.

After unloading our boats, I made the coffee, boiled the hominy, and fried the bacon and dried venison, which formed our staples of food, over a fire of "cabbage roots," or dry leaf stalks from the palm-trees, while Lefils erected the mosquito canopies, each supported by four stout stakes, and prepared our beds of palm leaves. These mosquito canopies are indispensable in South Florida, and form a portion of the outfit of every traveller. They are made of cheese-cloth, are generally six feet long, four wide, and three in height, so that in reality they are airy little tents, and afford excellent protection against the heavy night dews as well as against mosquitoes.

After supper, with pipes alight, and stretched at ease on our blan-kets, with the fire blazing brightly between us, Lefils and I exchanged anecdotes of hunting adventures, and from him I learned more of alli-gators and their ways than I had been taught by an experience of months of hunting in Floridian wilds. I shall never forget one of the stories he told me that night. It was of the tragic death of an acquain-tance of his, named G,, on the upper Suwanee River. Told with dramatic force by the hunter, with the necessary surroundings of that camp, and the bellowings of the great bull alligators sounding in our ears, it was absolutely blood-curdling.

It seems that G, who was a powerful man, weighing one hundred and eighty pounds, went out bird hunting with two friends, the party being only armed with shot guns. On their return, as they crossed the river, one proposed that they take a bath. Going a few rods below the

Shooting gators at close range, 1880s.
Credit: Florida State Archives

bridge to where there was a deep pool, they took their bath, left the water, and were dressing, when G, declared that he must have one more plunge. He dived from the bank into the deep water, re-appeared on the surface, and suddenly with a terrific shriek and a desperate struggle, again disappeared. A moment later a huge alligator rose to the surface, holding the man in his awful jaws, and swam leisurely toward the opposite bank of the river.

The monster had seized the swimmer by the right arm and the middle of his body, so that he was perfectly helpless. As poor G was thus borne across the river he begged in his agony that if his companions could not save him, they should shoot him; but with only their shot guns loaded with bird shot they were helpless and were forced to listen to the heart-rending appeals without the ability to render him the slightest service. They did, however, run up to the bridge, cross the river, and run down the other side, prepared to attack the brute with their knives and clubbed guns.

He in the meantime had reached the bank, dragged his whole length out upon it, and lay there for a minute with lifted head, and holding his victim, still alive and struggling, though horribly crushed and mangled high in the air. Suddenly alarmed by the approach of the men from the bridge, he turned, and with that quickness of motion so wonderful in these ungainly creatures plunged into the river, and with his doomed victim disappeared beneath the surface to rise no more. When the breathless runners reached the spot, a few bubbles floating on the blood-stained water were all that was left to tell of the hideous tragedy just enacted.

By daylight our little camp was astir, and a few minutes later was pervaded by the grateful aroma of boiling coffee and the odor of sizzling bacon. That day was occupied in building a hut, which we thatched with palm leaves, and making other preparations for our week's hunt. At odd times during the day the hunter shot a number of cormorants, and caught a quantity of cat-fish, all of which he threw into the river to attract alligators to the vicinity of our camp. He also carefully cleaned his rifles, a beautiful Winchester and an old muzzle-loading Jaeger, upon which he placed his chief reliance, and overhauled his harpoon, making for it a new shaft of tough hickory, and testing every inch of the fine Manilla line attached to the iron head.   This line, by the way, would be easily bitten in twain by the 'gator into whose body the harpoon had been driven were it not for an ingenious device of the hunter, who uses for the last six or eight feet of his line a bunch of strong hempen cords, which slip between the teeth of the animal, and baffle all his efforts at parting them. And, last of all, Lefils carefully cleaned and trimmed his bull's eye lantern; for all our hunting was to be what is known as "fire-hunting," and was to be done at night.

At last, the sun set, and almost immediately, for there is little twilight in those latitudes, came the darkness which we needed for our work. We ate our supper leisurely, however, and waited until about eight o'clock, "so as to give all the 'gators a chance to get out and be feeding," said the hunter. By that time it seemed to me as though all the alligators in the river were not only "out," but in the vicinity of our camp; for the cormorant and cat-fish bait had done its work, and it appeared little short of suicidal to venture out on the water in the black-ness of the night amongst the monsters that we could hear splashing, grunting, and occasionally bellowing like angry bulls, apparently within a few feet of us, and I confess I felt rather "scary" as I took my seat in the stern-sheets of the skiff, and with paddle in hand prepared to send her forth into their midst; but with Lefils it was a matter of regular busi-ness, and he was so collected and matter of fact that I quickly regained confidence.

He sat in the bow, rifle in hand, and with the bull's-eye lantern fastened by a leathern thong to his head. As the skiff shot out into the river, under the strokes of my broad-bladed paddle, she seemed to follow a golden path made by the narrow gleam of light, which was so bright and sharply defined that the darkness was like black walls on either side.

We went down stream, and I had not taken a dozen strokes before a sharp "hist" from the hunter caused me to cease paddling, and for a few seconds our boat drifted with the current, as noiselessly as an autumn leaf, down the bright water path. The gleam of his rifle barrel as Lefils raised it to his shoulder was followed by the sharp report, and a tremendous splashing in the water just ahead of us. But the bullet had done its work surely, and had crashed into the thick skull, plump between the eyes. The alligator sank, but with the long slender shaft of the harpoon we quickly found him, and the sharp barbed iron was driven deep into his scaly body. A slight effort brought him to the surface, his specific gravity being but little greater than that of water, and in another minute the hunter had dexterously lodged the ungainly carcass in the boat.

Within five minutes after the firing of the rifle-shot the harpoon had been detached from the dead body, and we were quietly paddling up stream in search of another. Within an hour two boat-loads of dead alligators, ten in all, had been killed, secured and deposited on the little bunch of tussocks, about a quarter of a mile below our camp, that had been selected as our skinning ground. Here we pulled them ashore and piled them in a heap to be operated upon the next day, or after they had become "thoroughly dead," as Lefils said.

All this time I had not seen a single alligator until after he had been shot, and was very anxious to "shine" a pair of eyes. So after we had piled our 'gators on the tussocks, the bull's eye was fastened to my head, and with rifle in hand I took my place in the bow of the boat, and Lefils took [it] that I had occupied . . . the stern. As we pulled out into the stream, I moved my head slowly from side to side, as directed by the hunter, and for a few minutes saw nothing save the shining pathway among the dark lily-pads.

Suddenly there flashed out from the blackness, right ahead, what appeared [to be] two lights shining at a great distance from us. They were of a dark lurid red, and glowed like dull coals of fire. I was about to call Lefil's attention to them, and ask what they were, when they moved slightly, and like an electric shock the knowledge flashed across me that a huge 'gator lay directly in our path, not more than twenty feet away, and that he was steadfastly regarding us, without showing the slightest disposition to move.

With a "hist" I arrested the progress of the boat, but not until she had drifted so close to the great motionless brute that the end of my rifle barrel almost touched the glowing eyes as I aimed between them and pulled the trigger. The report was followed by such a terrible lashing of the water under our bows that as the boat was swiftly backed from the scene of disturbance she was tossed like a cockle shell, and I experienced the same sensation as when, years before, I had been forced to sit quietly in the stern-sheets of a boat from which a keen-edged lance had just sent a monster whale into his death flurry.

As we lay beyond the sweep of the terrible tail, watching the death struggle of the huge reptile, Lefils said, disapprovingly: "That was a bad shot. You fired too quick. You didn't kill him half dead enough." It was very evident that I had not "killed him dead enough"; but his motions were so rapid and the light so uncertain that I had no chance to complete the deadening by another shot, and we were forced to wait patiently until he should become exhausted by his struggles.

He did not attempt to move from the place in which we had found him, but circled round and round, now raising his horrid head high into the air, and then lashing the water into a turbid foam with his powerful tail. This state of affairs lasted for ten or fifteen minutes, and then the great reptile sank out of sight, and a few ripples only marked the scene of the recent commotion.

"We can't afford to lose him; he's too big," said the hunter as he picked up his harpoon, and we again exchanged places.

A few minutes careful feeling among the bonnet roots, and then the barbed iron was driven downward with the full force of the sinewy arm, and as I backed the boat, Lefils seized his rifle. At the same instant there was a rush through the water, and by the light of the bull's-eye, which still remained on my head, I had a vision of wide-open jaws and gleaming teeth. Just as they were about to close upon me, or so it seemed, there came a shot, a rending of wood, and I found myself struggling in the dark waters of the river, the lantern extinguished, and everything shrouded in deepest blackness.

As I stood irresolute in water up to my shoulders, a vigorous stream of the most unique oaths from out of the darkness indicated the presence of the 'gator-hunter. I found that he still held his rifle in his hand, and as his cartridges were water-proof, our predicament was not so alarming nor our loss as serious as had at first appeared. But we were forced to wait until daylight before attempting the recovery of our boat. We waded to the bank, and found ourselves on the tussocks in company with our victims of the earlier hours of our hunt. Although they were supposed to be dead 'gators, and had been left there as such, several of them showed such unmistakable signs of life as we left the river and crawled out amongst them that they had to be "killed again," as Lefils said. He did not waste ammunition on them, but killed them with his hunting knife, in each case reaching across the animal, and driving the long knife into the body just back of the fore-shoulder.

The "why" of this method of procedure was so evident that no questions nor explanations were needed, for the instant the alligator felt the knife, he struck so savagely in the direction from which he supposed the blow to have come, with both head and tail, that had the hunter stood on that side he would have received serious if not fatal injury. Having thus effectually quieted our companions in this our enforced lodging-place, we seated ourselves on one of the scaly bodies, and prepared to pass the hours until daylight as comfortably as possible. The tobacco and matches in my water-proof pouch proved of inestimable value, and in the glowing bowls of our pipes we found a source of cheerfulness which even our wet garments, made cooler and wetter by the damp night breeze, could not extinguish.

We also succeeded in relighting the bull's-eye lantern, which was very fortunate, for by its light we discovered and killed a number of venomous water-moccasins which had invaded the tussocks, probably only on speculative visits of inquiry, but possibly with murderous intent. I am not sure, however, that they were not attracted by the light, for in all my six months' experience of camp life in Florida I have never been troubled by snakes, and doubt very much if they will, unprovoked, attack a man. Our light also attracted several alligators, whose curiosity was repaid by bullets, and whose dead bodies we obtained next day. Had it not been for the clouds of mosquitoes that enveloped us, our night with the 'gators would have been comparatively comfortable, but they drove us to the verge of insanity, and the first streaks of dawn were hailed with delight.

As soon as it became sufficiently light for us to pick our way, we succeeded, partly by wading and partly by swimming, in regaining our camp, where our thorough enjoyment of dry clothes, hot coffee, and a hearty breakfast almost compensated for the discomforts and dangers of the preceding hours. In my canoe we repaired to the scene of our disaster, and found our enemy of the night before floating on his back, his white belly glistening in the sunlight, stone-dead, and still attached to the sunken skiff by the line, of which one end was fast to the harpoon in his body and the other to the bow of the boat.

It seems that, when he made his final rush at us, Lefils had fired a ball down the yawning chasm of his throat, and that in his death agony the alligator had seized the side of the boat, and torn it off from stem to stern. We dragged him up on the tussocks, and measured him, finding him to be within an inch of thirteen feet long. Although during that week we killed one hundred and twenty alligators, no one of them equalled him in size, nor did we have any serious trouble with any other during the hunt.

After eight days' hard work we abandoned our comfortable camp, and with heavily laden boats turned our faces up the river toward Fort Bassinger and the civilization which lay beyond.

Alligator Shooting in Florida

by John Mortimer Murphy

The following extract from a very long article, which appeared in Outing *for December (1899, pp. 353–64), discusses the evolution of crocodiles and alligators, as well as the protective instinct on the part of alligator mothers toward their young. It also deals with differences between alligators and crocodiles, as well as the experience of hunting gators in various parts of Florida. Among the terms to be explained are* congener—*a related animal;* plethoric—*having a superabundance of blood in the system;* aldermanic—*like an alderman, i.e. very big;* Caloosahatchee—*a river in southwestern Florida.*

A ccording to the book of Genesis the waters brought forth the fish and the birds, and according to paleontologists that book is correct, the reptiles being the source from which emanated our feathered creation. Birds are, therefore, simply modified saurians, the scales of the latter having become transformed into feathers on the former, and the fore feet into wings. How many eons it took to make this wonderful transformation of mud-crawling, hideous reptiles into winged and beautiful songsters no scientist can determine. Yet that one is the product of the other is apparent to every student of primitive animal life. Look, for instance, at the picture of the ichthyosaurus, compare it with that of the bat-like reptile, the pterodactyl, and note how similar in form they are, though differing vastly in size, the former was finned reptile, twenty feet or more in length, the latter a winged reptile, about the size of a pigeon, which had teeth, and a long, pointed tail like that of a lizard. It was at this period of the earth's history that both forms of life began to form into distinct groups, and the divergence has been getting greater ever since, until, at present, few persons besides students of zoology would think that one bore any relationship to the other. The penguin is probably the nearest living type of the pterodactyl, and the crocodile and alligator of the ichthyosaurus.

It may not be generally known that both the crocodile and alligator are denizens of Floridian waters, but such is the fact. The former is more southern in its habitat than the latter, and also shows a more marked preference for running streams and sandy beaches near the seashore. Its favorite ground for a siesta is a sloping beach which commands a good view of the environments. When alarmed it dashes into the rolling billows, should any be near, for it is far more marine in its habits than its congener, and swims boldly into the open sea. It is evidently capable of making long voyages, for it has been found among the keys of the Florida Reef, having, apparently, reached them from Cuba. Many persons in this State, well acquainted with the saurians, cannot tell an alligator from a crocodile; yet each has distinctive traits so well marked that a single glance is enough to enable an expert to distinguish them apart.

The alligator has, in the first place, a shorter snout, a broader head, and more teeth than its congener. It does not possess the two holes in the upper jaw into which the two great tusks of the lower jaw fit, which are so prominent a characteristic of the latter, nor do the teeth protrude through the upper jaw, as they do in the crocodile. A glance at the snout will therefore enable a novice to tell whether the saurian he espies is an alligator or a crocodile.

Two species, or varieties, of the former are supposed to be residents of Florida, one being known as the black and the other as the brown alligator. The first, which is quite plethoric, if not aldermanic, in proportions, ranges from eight to thirteen or more feet in length, and makes its home in the bank of some sluggish stream, cosy lagoon, tranquil lake, and saw-grass savanna, while the second is attached to rapid rivers, its favorite haunts being deep pools, sheltering crags or bushes, and sandy banks. It also frequents brackish streams, which the first generally avoids, and is, on the whole, longer, more slender, quicker, and more active than its congener, and seems to have no objection to the sea, to which it often makes trips during the fishing season in August, September and October. I have found both varieties, for I do not consider them distinct enough to be classed as species, at the mouths of rivers emptying into the Gulf of Mexico as far south as the Caloosahatchee, their place on the lower keys being occupied by crocodiles.

I do not recall any scene more expressive of hideous horror than a mangrove morass swarming with ferocious mosquitoes, filthy-looking saurians, and slimy snakes of various hues, whose lightest sting is as fatal as a dose of prussic acid, while the deadly miasma which fills the air is quite palpable. It is fortunate that such spots are infrequent, and more so that they are difficult of approach, for they are usually located amid a dense mass of green shrubbery, which shows light and life above and gloom and death below.

The nests of the crocodiles and alligators look much alike, the main difference being in size. The former commence building their nurseries as early as June, and the latter from July to August, the dates varying according to the character of the weather and their northern or southern habitat. It is only the female of each species which engages in architecture, and, primitive as that may be, she works at it with a persistence and determination most worthy of praise until her domicile is completed. Her first movement is to fill her mouth with dead leaves, grass, shrubs or wet soil, and carry them to where she intends to build her nest.

After laying the foundation, which has a diameter of six or seven feet, she piles her material carefully by using her head as a trowel, and sometimes her forepaws. When the walls are from four to seven feet high she opens a hole in the top and drops her eggs, separating them into layers by means of earth, dry grass and leaves, and when all are laid she covers them with another layer of the same material, arranging it carefully, in order to make it as protective as possible. This done, she retires to a convenient shelter close by, leaving her eggs to be hatched by the heat of the sun and the steam arising from decaying vegetation.

The eggs are about as large as those of an ordinary goose, have a decidedly musky odor, and, like those of all reptilia, have a tough, membraneous covering instead of a shell. They are eagerly devoured by bears, pumas, wild cats, cranes, herons, and other furred and feathered enemies, but if they secure them it is only when the female is absent or sleeping, for she will fight any living thing in defense of her nest. Each nursery contains between forty and eighty eggs, and, as nearly all prove fertile, it is quite evident that the country would swarm with the saurians unless Nature placed a check on their numbers. These checks are numerous enough, and embrace fur, fin and feather. Moccasin snakes, darters or water turkeys, members of the *Grallidae*, and many species of fish prey on them constantly, but their worst enemy is, in all probability, the male alligator, for he will devour all the young in a nest in a few minutes. The mother knows this only too well, hence she seldom strays far from her nursery, and when the youngsters announce their birth, by vehement croaking, she is generally the first to answer their summons and escort them from their prison. On emerging from this retreat she leads them to water immediately, and carefully watches over their

---

welfare until the following November or December, when all separate to hibernate during the cold weather.

As soon as a male alligator hears the cries of the juveniles he becomes exceedingly alert, and steals toward the nursery with all the cautiousness of his nature, for he knows full well what is in store for him should the female discover him while on his cannibalistic expedition. If he finds the coast clear he hastily tears open the nest with jaw and paws, and devours as he digs; yet, no matter how thoroughly he may be enjoying his feast, he retreats in the most ludicrously precipitate manner on seeing the female approach. The latter often pursues him until he seeks refuge in the water or his home in the bank of a contiguous pond or stream; but should she overtake him she attacks him with the utmost fury, using teeth and tail with extraordinary effect, and generally routing him or leaving him badly crippled. An assault on her progeny drives all timidity from her nature, and she is then as ready to face a man as a mouse. I have never known an alligator to pursue a...hunter over land and through water except when defending her young; in all other instances that I recall, the saurian, when brought to bay, was only too glad to escape, if it had the opportunity.

An acquaintance of mine once fired at an alligator which he saw

Nap time.
Credit: Florida State Archives

Alligators have captured people's imaginations in Florida since before Ponce de León arrived here as the first European tourist in 1513. Across Florida, alligator attractions, like Gatorland in Orlando, cater to our unending fascination with animals-that-can-eat-you.

Gators are adapted for moving in water with their powerful tails, and are also capable of running in short bursts at surprising speeds with their short, stocky legs.

A baby gator surveys its world from atop its mother's head. Crocodilians, unlike almost all other reptiles, are protective of their young. Parents are attracted to pods of young alligators by the distinctive vocalizations of their hatchlings. Baby gators often use adults as basking platforms to get out of flooded vegetation and to gain body heat in the sun.

Ten-inch-long baby alligators hatch out after about 65 days and stay close to Mom for about six months. The babies will eat insects, crustaceans, and small fish if they can catch them, but they must be mindful that their mothers can be cannibalistic.

Above: Alligator eyes are among nature's most intriguing.
Right: Basking gators crowd for a spot in the sun at the St. Augustine Alligator Farm. **Below:** Alligators, egrets, and herons make for a delicate balance at Paynes Prairie State Preserve in Gainesville, one of the finest natural alligator viewing areas in America. Florida's first state preserve, Paynes Prairie is home to several thousand alligators.

Above left: Lying in wait, the alligator sits atop the food chain as a snowy egret feeds on a fish at the St. Augustine Alligator Farm. Alligators scare away egg-stealing predators like raccoons and opossums. Since alligators don't climb trees, the birds are comfortable with the symbiotic arrangement. **Left:** A young alligator contemplates a meal. After slowly inching across the lily pad at Paynes Prairie, the alligator lunged forward and swallowed the dragonfly. **Above:** At Gatorland, visitors pose for a memorable take-home photo in the jaws of a lifelike gator.

"Party Your Tail Off" was the aptly-named theme for King Gator's Fundango at Universal Studios. With a Mardi Gras flavor, a nightly beach parade through the Orlando theme park culminated with the passing of the 75-foot-long King Gator.

Long before Disney forever changed Orlando, Gatorland was there, pulling in the tourists to get an up-close-and-personal view of thousands of Florida's famous gators. The entrance to Gatorland is classic kitsch that has enlivened the photo albums of tourists from Kansas City to Katmandu.

The Skin Shop in Alachua County markets a wide array of alligator products, including back scratchers, belts, wallets, and decorative desk and wall mounts and curios. The shop wholesales to 2,000 stores worldwide.

Pam and Bill Feaster have come to enjoy the alligators at their Newnan's Lake home. So when they were searching for a Florida motif to use during a recent remodeling, it seemed only right to invite a ceramic gator into the pool.

Matt Bradshaw knew he wanted to do something big in retirement, and he has . . . big and green. Matt and his wife, Kathy, took two years and two tons of steel to craft this one-of-a-kind barbecue grill that was displayed in the University of Florida homecoming parade. But this is no ordinary float. The belly of the beast opens to a three-by-eight-foot grill which can handle up to 300 pounds of burgers and ribs—and gator tail steaks.

Albert and Alberta are proud symbols of the athletic prowess of the University of Florida Gators, 1996 national college football champions.

Florida Governor Bob Martinez signed a resolution proclaiming the alligator to be Florida's official state reptile after Tallahassee schoolchildren proposed the designation.

Gil Castillo tours the Sunshine State wrestling alligators at county fairs. "Even though we're in gator country, please don't root for the gator," Castillo urges his audience.

Charlie Blythe's holiday display features 40,000 lights and one alligator. Go Gators!

A drought on Paynes Prairie forces an unusually dense concentration of alligators to gather in the only deep water remaining in the state preserve. Sun worshipers by day, alligators are more active after dark—feeding,

courting, bellowing, and piercing the nocturnal gloom with their powerful night vision. Low-power electronic flash illuminates their eyes during this 30-second time-exposure at dusk.

The allure of
alligators is
as deep as
our primal
fears. Like
dragons in
paradise,
alligators
remind us
that we are
just visitors
in the land
of wild and
original
Florida.

lying under a bush close to the river, and planted his bullet solidly in its side, but the reptile did not make the slightest move. He fired a second time with the same result. Thinking the animal was dead, he advanced rapidly and incautiously toward it with an empty rifle. On approaching to within fifteen or twenty feet of the saurian, he was horror stricken to see it charge open mouthed, and at a pace of which he thought it incapable. He had just time enough to glance at the spot the animal had quitted and note that it was covered with crawling, croaking little 'gators, before the musky hissing of the mother got so strong as to induce him to face about and dash for his boat, which was anchored about a hundred yards out in the stream on account of the shallowness of the water. He dashed through the bushes, sprawled through the muddy beach, and half ran and half swam through the river, after throwing away his rifle, but the enraged reptile still pursued him, its eyes being of a greenish-red hue and gleaming with the most demoniacal hatred.

Running and terror combined had so exhausted the fugitive that he was unable to clamber into the boat after reaching it, and there is every probability that he would have fallen a prey to the infuriated brute had not his comrade promptly "yanked" him in on finding him hanging listlessly to the side. A couple of bullets sent the motherly saurian hurriedly shoreward, where she rejoined her squalling offspring and led them to a place of greater security. The fugitive picked up his rifle when the mother disappeared, and vowed to never again go gunning for alligators without a full magazine. This incident strongly impressed him with the fact that an alligator is not as stupid as it looks, nor so slow as its ungainly legs would indicate.

Another female alligator attacked a horse and rider while crossing a stream because they frightened the youngsters in her company. The horse was so badly injured about the hind legs that he was hardly able to reach dry land. The rider on seeing this was rendered so furious that he went to a farm house close by, borrowed an axe, and wading to his arm pits into the river, boldly assaulted the reptile. He swung his weapon much as a Crusader his battle axe among the Saracens, and, although the saurian used all her skill and power in defending herself and progeny, she was killed in less than ten minutes, her skull being broken in several places. She was then towed ashore, and left there as a feast for the buzzards. The horse subsequently recovered, but it was many a day before he was fit for service.

Tales of this sort could be extended into a volume, but I think those related are sufficient to prove that a female alligator is no mean foe when she is trying to protect her offspring.

In passing through low, swampy lands in summer, persons should reconnoitre the ground carefully, as several nests are frequently found close together in such places, and some are so carefully concealed that one cannot tell their character until he is in their midst. If his presence is then detected by the lurking mothers, he is liable to be charged from various directions simultaneously, and if he does not prove nimble of foot and quick of eye, he is in danger of bearing the impression of some brute's tail on his leg for many a day.

A Northern Girl's "Huntin' of a Gaitah"

by Marion Pryde Quay

This account of an alligator hunt, which was published in Outing
Magazine *(February 1900, pp. 439–443), is quite different from the
arduous and extended hunt described in* Alligator Hunting with
Seminoles *by Kirk Munroe. Englishman Izaak Walton (1593–1683), who
is mentioned in the article, wrote a famous book about fishing,* The
Compleat Angler. *The following terms might be unclear to modern
readers:* factotum—*a Jack of all trades;* Nimrod—*a hunter; and* mustang—
a former wild horse of the Western prairies.

Within the memory of the middle-aged "Crackers," as the
natives are called, the vast pine-lands of Florida were
seamed and threaded with countless trails leading over the
grass-grown marshes from one "alligator hole" to another. Now one
seldom finds them, and a big alligator is a rare discovery.

This sudden disappearance is owing chiefly to the Seminole Indian.
Florida is his "happy hunting ground." Where a white man cannot go,
he lives and thrives. He is a nomad, and all through the pine-lands one
finds the ashes of his camp-fire, the ridge-pole of his dismantled tent,
signs always that the country about has been hunted over, and the "alligator holes" robbed of their booty.

Alligator skins are the Seminole's chief article of barter. They are
brought in for miles and traded at the scattered country stores for
gaudily colored bandanna handkerchiefs—which are made into a sort
of turban—beads, ammunition, knives, etc.; and owing to this near-by
depletion the "sob of the 'gator" grows less in the land.

With the disappearing of the alligator comes an added zest to the
hunt. It lends difficulty to the already existing danger and difficulty.
Danger and the charm of coming close to Nature, with all her mysteries
and moods, are the magnets which for countless ages have drawn men
forth from the haunts of men, to slay and spare not.

S—L— on the Indian River is a settlement of about a dozen houses.

SHOOTING ALLIGATORS.

Shooting gators from a steamer on the Oklawaha River, 1874.
Credit: Florida State Archives

To the right are a few low cottages given over each year to the Northern followers of Izaak Walton, who come South in search of tarpon and winter fishing. In front the wide lovely Indian River stretches away, fringed with palms and weird mangrove trees and pulsing to every heart-beat of the ocean. At the other points of the compass the "Florida Cracker" hath his habitation, and flourisheth like a green bay tree.

It was from one of our house party, Clarence, our guide, fisherman and general factotum, that I learned that here one might go a "huntin' of a 'gaitah" with a reasonable hope of finding one.

One morning I had wandered down to the dock before breakfast and was leaning over the railing, drawing in long breaths of fresh morning air, and viewing the heavens with a would-be fisherman's eye for any sign unfavorable to the plans we had made for the day. Clarence was polishing up the boats and arranging the fishing tackle. The weather was calm and hot and sunshiny, and the river lay so motionless and still that one could hear the faint splash of leaping fish and mark where they had fallen.

"Good morning, Clarence," I called. "A good day for Spanish mackerel; no breeze and no clouds. I think we can count on rare sport out at sea."

Clarence stood still and surveyed the horizon carefully.

"A good day fo' mack'rel, suah, Miss," he said, "and you all suah to get lots of fish; but hit's a bettah day, by fah, fo' 'gaitahs.'"

I examined Clarence carefully for any sign of suppressed amusement, a faintest trace of guile.

"Alligator-hunting, Clarence," I said blandly; "and where would one find them? Here? In the river?"

"Not yere, Miss," Clarence laughed amusedly. "Inland huntin' fo' 'gaitahs. Too much salt yere, tho' they do come occasional'. Th'ah some of 'em back in th' country, big uns. You all'd ought to go a huntin' of 'em. I can c'yar yo' wheah yo' suah get a 'gaitah,'" and Clarence sat down and mused.

He told me stories of 'gators and 'gator hunts, of hair-breadth escapes and odd experiences, until the breakfast bell rang, and I hurried away, filled with a desire to enroll myself in the lists of those valiant hunters who "seek the bubble reputation, even at the alligator's mouth." Reputation there would be, should we be fortunate. I discovered that of twenty men who had gone alligator-hunting from the settlement in the last two years, only two had been successful. My thirst for the fray fired my cousin, V—, to an answering enthusiasm, and she decided to go with me as aid and general voucher for all the tales I hoped to tell when we came back. We had several protracted meetings with Clarence in the next few days, and discussed plans and probabilities with a delightful sense of mystery.

There are two ways to hunt alligators. One is to take a small boat and a guide and row up one of the fresh-water streams. Here, lying flat down in the bottom of the boat in the broiling sun, with your rifle cocked and ready for instant action, you calmly allow the mosquitoes to devour you, while you strain your eyes in the blinding light and patiently watch for two little diamond points on the water and maybe a tiny rough place—not larger than your hand—for that is what your alligator will look like if you see him. Clarence told me that he went out for four successive days with one man, and each day they lay in the sun for hours at a time and never caught a glimpse of a 'gator. Then the man tired of the sport.

The other and more dangerous way is to drive out to the "alligator holes," where an encounter with a 'gator becomes almost a hand-to-hand fight, as you are on foot and actually in the same water with him. Altogether, at the "holes," one needs a cooler head, and good marksmanship is a necessity. On the latter score, fortunately, I had not much hesitation as I had shot more or less all my life, and knew that I could depend upon the accuracy of my aim.

Inland hunting in the end proved more attractive, and having decided this important question, we arranged with Clarence and with Aiden, his brother—who is a veritable Nimrod—to go with us, provide a conveyance, etc. Then and not until then, we laid our plans before the house party, who amused themselves for the remainder of the evening launching at us dainty shafts of sarcasm and sparkling witticisms, which left us inwardly saddened, but outwardly, most valiant and bold.

The morning of our hunt dawned bright and lovely, and at nine the guides were waiting for us with a two-seated wagon and a "one-time" mustang. They had with them a gun to shoot any moccasin we might encounter, a huge flask of whiskey as an antidote for snake-bites, and two long poles and hooks to land our alligator. We added a kodak, to photograph the spoils, and my rifle and ammunition. I used a Winchester repeating rifle of the '92 model, with 38-caliber, long-distance cartridges.

We drove back into the country for about a mile, over a sandy uninteresting road, which grew suddenly lovely as we reached a small stream, one of the many that drain the swamps. There was a big alligator track along one bank, a long, wet-looking streak through the sand, which Clarence pointed out, and the spirits of hunts-women awoke within us and our hearts beat high! Evidently we were on the trail.

Following the little stream, we drove directly through the pine forest, where the ground was thickly overgrown with palmettos, and came out upon a big, swampy, grassy space, with a circle of willows in the center—our first "alligator hole."

The "alligator holes" are at once curious and lovely. All through the pine-lands there runs a network of marshy ground covered with shallow swamp water and overgrown with tall, willowy, saw-grass. Here and there the waters deepen into little open ponds, and to these the name "alligator hole" is given. The name really refers to the holes the alligators tunnel out in the bottom of the pond, and into which they creep when startled. Here they can lie, safely stowed away, for hours without coming to the surface for air. The ponds are covered with water-lilies and fringed about with willows, which stand out boldly against the wide, flat monotony of the swamps and are very pictur-esque. Each hole should boast two or three alligators and many tiny ones; and its waters, together with the waters of the swamp around it, are infested with moccasins, only a little less deadly than the Southern rattlesnake.

Clarence and Aiden went to reconnoiter for game. They shot two moccasins not two feet away from us, and we saw some fifteen others, but no alligator; so we stowed the snakes away in the wagon as trophies and set off for another hole. We reached it after an hour's driving, and Clarence went again to look for alligators. He disappeared in the grass, and we could see his head now and again above it. As we reached the hole a flock of blue heron rose from the willows and sailed away, and a white owl cut the air with its lonely cry. We felt how small a part of creation we were in the wilderness, it all looked so wide and lonely, the swamp and all around us pathless forest.

The guide came back in a few moments, all excitement. He had discovered an alligator. He had crept in quite close to the pool without seeing a sign of our quarry, and had just risen to shout to me that there were none to be found, when a huge one, which he had failed to see, and which was sunning itself among the lily pads, jumped out and snapped at him. The boy still looked rather white and shaky. He had thrown himself back on the grass to escape, and the alligator had sunk.

"A fo'teen-foot 'gaitah, *suah*."

I was to come at once.

I came—I jumped out of the wagon into two feet of cold, oozy swamp water, put a dozen cartridges into my rifle and waded off through the swamp, with V— diligently waving good wishes in the distance.

Clarence kept a close lookout for snakes, and we slipped along as quietly as one can slip through saw-grass, taller than your head, and water which is one moment deep and the next shallow. Finally we reached the hole and I stood and looked at it and felt that cold wave of excitement go over me, which shivers up and down your back and tingles to your very finger-tips. This was alligator-hunting! The black pool of water held all sorts of possibilities for me, and I watched and waited with bated breath.

I waited a long time. I was growing disheartened and weary before I finally saw an alligator; and yet, when he did come, he came so quietly that it was with a little shock of surprise that I looked across the pool and saw him slyly peeping out from beneath a lily leaf. There had been no faintest sound, not the slightest ripple on the water, but there he was. I could just see his eyes, two bright spots, and could imagine his long, dark shape beneath the water. My longing to fire was scarcely controllable and my fingers fairly trembled on the trigger of my rifle; but I was so afraid he might be small and that I might frighten away my big "'gaitah" by the report, if I shot, that I sent the guide around the pool to discover his size. Clarence disappeared, and after what seemed an age of waiting, I saw him creep out on the other side, bend over—then he slipped and fell, and my "'gaitah" quietly sank. I could have wept bitter tears of disappointment. It was the big alligator and it would have been such an easy shot. They tried to bring him up again by imitating the sob of an alligator—"grunting him up," they call it—but in spite of all lures it was an hour before another one appeared. This time I was not too curious as to his size—I fired and he rolled his length over in the water, the inglorious length of three and a half feet!

What a fall was there, my countrymen! He was a "'gaitah," however, and better at least than none, so Clarence hooked him out, and as it was quite late, we waded off to the wagon and V—. That demure maiden, when she saw me, gave way to inexplicable and unrestrained mirth.

"My dear," she said, when she could, "do you mean to tell me you shot that *monster* in *those*?"

"*Those*" were my veil and gloves, and I had—shades of departed hunters forgive! —I had shot my first alligator in my gloves and veil; I was too much excited to notice them.

We drove slowly home after that, fully determined to come again; and over the renewed derision that greeted us upon our arrival I will charitably draw a veil.

That evening I sat on the front steps and plucked the burrs from my hunting skirt. This I did to show to all whom it might concern the supreme indifference with which I received the various wise saws leveled at me by "the party," who also sat on the front steps and were fast making life a burden to me.

Into this scene of agony, there came "Jeems" Ruggles.

"Jeems" Ruggles is our neighboring "Cracker" to the left, and he who knoweth not "Jeems" knoweth not S—L—. This evening he shambled barefooted out of his front gate, with his long, sunburned hair floating back from his brown face, his faded blue shirt widely open at the neck, his trousers short and equally faded, his shoes tied by their strings around his neck.

"Jeems" came along the beach and leaned on our front gate, and I welcomed his advent with joy. Here was relief!

"Good evening, Mr. Ruggles," I said, with a beaming smile.

"Jeems" smiled back as beamingly and swung on the gate.

"By gravvy, Miss Z—," he said, "I year yo' been 'gaitah huntin' this mahnin'!"

I received this remark in stony silence.

"And I year," "Jeems" continued as beamingly, "I year, yo' on'y got a no'count 'gaitah, and by gravvy, Miss Z—, it's too bad. I jest stopped to tell yo'—yo' bein' dis'pointed 'at way—'at my chillun they got a *pet* 'gaitah down yere in the rivah and they done got him tied to a stake; and, by gravvy! if yo' would like to shoot *him*—he cahn't get away, yo' know, no how, and whenst yo' miss him, yo' can jest fiah away some moah."

I rose and fled, and "the party" laughed loud and long. Mr. Ruggles may have meant well, but after that encounter *nothing* could have kept me from going out for alligators the next day!

We started at the same hour the next morning, and went directly to the farthest pool. When we arrived, Clarence and I crept up, talking in whispers, but there were no fresh trails and no alligators to be seen, except a tiny one, which Aiden caught and shook, head down, until its sobs of grief resounded over the water—all to no avail; and the guides, after examining the "hole," gave up any hope of getting me a quiet shot. The alligator had probably heard us as we crept through the saw-grass; and sunk, frightened, to its tunnel in the pool. The only thing left to do was to try to stir him up with a landing-hook, a dangerous proceeding. A long spiked hook is fastened to a heavy pole, and the entire pool is sounded. When the alligator is struck, he generally comes up with a headlong rush, which creates general havoc.

Clarence cautioned me to be ready to fire at once, as a minute's delay might be fatal, and to be careful in my aim, as I might, in my excitement, shoot him or Aiden. I steadied my nerves for serious work.

One may fire at an alligator half asleep and floating among lily pads, with stoical calm, if one is an experienced hunter; but when you know that the beast, if he comes at all, will come angry, open-mouthed and meaning fight; that he is big; that you are literally in the same water with him, and that water is his element and not yours—the situation yields matter for consideration. Aiden and Clarence prodded and pushed and pushed and prodded with their long spiked poles, but only stirred up lily stems and old logs. Finally, I grew wearied with the long nervous strain of watching, and was just about to call to Clarence to come away, when there was a splash! a yell!—they had struck him, and he came out with his enormous mouth wide open—with a hiss, a jump and a snap, breaking the poles and scattering everything right and left! He looked tremendous! I fired, and he rolled over on the water dead. An eight-and-a-half-foot 'gator, and I had shot him.

Oh, the rapture of it all! I laughed and shouted with delight! Then I stood off and surveyed his big bulk with feelings of pride and vainglory. Clarence's raptures were all for the shot. The bullet had struck the 'gator just between the eyes, and killed him instantly. The skull of an alligator is very thick, and there are just two small spots where one can hit and kill him—one is between the eyes, and the other, a side shot, is just beneath the ear.

The guides dragged the beast out, curled him up in the wagon, and covered him over with willow boughs, as he was a rather gory-looking object. We gave three ringing cheers and fired a salute, and then with infinite glee set off for S—L—. We fired other salutes as we drove in, and hearing them, "the party" gathered in amazement to receive us. Then the neighborhood assembled as the news of our exploit spread, and before them all we stretched out our eight-and-a-half-foot alligator and stood back with negligent ease to receive congratulations.

That evening, after dinner, "Jeems" Ruggles again swung on our front gate and again he beamed.

"Good evening, Miss Z—. By gravvy, I year yo' cert'ny got a 'gaitah."

I smiled graciously.

"And I jest stopped yere to say 'at I reckon my chillun kin keep thar pet 'gaitah, yo' won't want him *much*."

"I sha'n't want the 'gator, Mr. Ruggles, thank you," I said; "and tell your children for me, that if their live alligator brings them as much pleasure as my dead one has given me, they have a treasure and would better keep him." Then I smiled forgiveness on "the party," and "Jeems" betook himself off.

We started North the next morning, and Clarence surprised and delighted me by appearing with the skin of my alligator, which he had taken off at night that I might have it to take home with me. He brought me, too, the bullet I had used. The entire settlement gathered to see us off, and as we stood at the back of our car waiting for the express to come and carry us away, we felt very much lionized.

Our train came at last. The car was coupled on with a bump, and we waved good-bye to our "Cracker" friends. As we moved, the last words we heard were, from Clarence: "Come down next yeah, Miss Z—, and I'll give yo' a shot at a beah"; from Aiden, "Come down and shoot a wile-cat."

I have my alligator skin tanned as a trophy, I have my memories— a constantly recurring pleasure—and I am going back to add to my experiences a "beah hunt" with Clarence and a shot at a "wile-cat" with Aiden.

I have thoroughly enjoyed my "Cracker" friends. While they are a law unto themselves, this is a quality that develops in the people of any unreclaimed, thinly settled country. It springs up of necessity—in self-defense. I found them always manly, courteous, kind-hearted, and full of resources for the furthering of any pleasure we might plan. They have a rich vein of natural, original humor, and are brave with an unconscious fearlessness most attractive. We felt that we were safe with them always, under any circumstances—even in the midst of the dangers attending the "huntin' of a 'gaitah."

The Passing of the Florida Alligator

by A.W. Dimock

This story, which appeared in Harper's Magazine *(April 1908, pp. 669–676), gives a different perspective to the plight of the alligator. Dimock, who was born in Nova Scotia in 1842 and died in 1918, was an early environmentalist who saw the need to save the alligator from extinction. He wrote such works as* Florida Enchantments *(1908) and* The Book of the Tarpon *(1911).*

The alligator has always been the picturesque and popular feature of the peninsula of Florida. He enlivened its waters, made his bed on the banks of its streams, and, seconded by flocks of snowy heron and other birds of beauty and grace which burdened the trees and filled the air, started the tide of travel that sends fifty thousand tourists to the coast and rivers of Florida each year. The plumes of the egrets adorn the hats of the women; the tourist has murdered the birds that beckoned him. Therefore to the few surviving alligators attaches the credit of creating a northern State on the border of the tropics.

This creature has served as a target for every rifle that was ever brought into the State and deserves to be put to a better use. The alligator, as I have known him, or at least a few thousand of him, is as harmless as a cow; even more so, for the Florida cow has been known to kill folks, while the Florida alligator never harmed a human being, outside of some imaginative newspaper. I have swum without trepidation rivers in Florida which abounded in alligators, but never crossed a meadow containing Florida cattle without palpitation of the heart.

In the long ago, before dry plates made a sportsman weapon of the camera, or the voice of the nature-lover had been raised in the land, I hunted the alligator, and, *mea culpa*, slew many of his family for sport. Day after day I was rowed down the romantic Homosassa, from the fountain from which it springs, through Hell Gate to Shell Island at its mouth; past islands of palmetto, and between banks of red cedar and live oak festooned with Spanish moss; over water alive with leaping fish and covered with solid acres of duck and other water fowl; in air heavy with the odor of magnolia and orange blossoms and sweet with the fragrance of jessamine. My boatman rowed lazily while, half asleep, I scanned the surface of the river through glasses until I saw floating upon it the three dark dots made by the nose and eyes of the reptile I sought. I awoke suddenly from my dreams, and, as gradually the boat approached and silently the alligator sank into the depths, selected the shadow of some near-by bank, and waited patiently, rifle in hand, for his reappearance. In from five to thirty minutes a black spot appeared upon the brilliant surface of the stream, just as a whispered warning from the keen-eyed oarsman reached me. Slowly the rifle was raised, my cheek rested lovingly upon its stock, a fine bead was drawn on the bump back of the reptile's eye, and a bullet tore through the brain of the brute, a yellow belly was upturned and pathetic paws uplifted. There followed a quick dash of the skiff through the water as the boatman bent to the oars, for the creature was due to sink in a minute, and unless I grabbed a paw before he went down I might have to fish for him an hour or more with hook and pole in the depths. After hauling the carcass aboard the skiff, I counted the incident closed; but once it happened that the game had only begun, and there was another inning, with the reptile at the bat. One moment I was looking upon an alligator lying dead in the bottom of the boat, with his tail in the bow, his body under the seat of the oarsman, and his closed jaws pointed at me as I sat in the stern. The next instant the big mouth, with its double row of great, gleaming ivory teeth, was wide open and advancing as fast as the reptile could paddle his huge body toward me. The boatman yelled as he grabbed a hind leg of the brute, without staying his progress an instant, while I jumped to my feet, stood for a moment on the seat in the stern, and when the mouth of the alligator was within a few inches of my legs, dove into the river.

Sportsmen and tourists have done what evil they could, but the deadly foe of the alligator, the implement that has nearly compassed his extinction and driven him from every river and lake on the coast, is the bull's-eye lantern. Its glare hypnotizes and holds helpless the reptile, as the gleaming eye of the snake is reputed to fascinate (but probably doesn't) the fluttering bird. Fire hunting for alligators, as a business, is butchery, bloody and revolting. Yet the sportsman's first fire hunt with firearms, and it should be his last, is all romance and thrill, until the last bloody act.

I first bound the bull's-eye upon my own forehead when in camp beside an inland salt water lake in South Florida. Because of lack of

An alligator hunt in the 1870s.
Credit: Florida State Archives

padding or a skull too thin, the lantern bruised my head and blistered my brain, but the pictures painted that night remain bright in my memory. I crouched in the bow with my rifle beside me as the captain sculled the skiff across the end of the lake and into a narrow creek, the mouth of which was hidden by bushes. We cut away tangles of vines and dragged the skiff under branches and over roots, lighted only by the single beam from the lamp on my forehead. As we emerged into a small open pond, a loud *Whoo-hoo-hoo* from the thick foliage over my head was answered from out of the darkness across the pond. The silence that followed was broken a minute later by the distant cry of a panther. The skiff was motionless, and as I let the beam of light from the lantern stray over the calm surface of the lake and play among the roots of the mangroves on its border, I saw a reptile in each lump of mud and twisted tree trunk. Then, as the skiff glided silently along the shore, the

A successful gator hunt in the 1890s.
Credit: Florida State Archives

soft step of a wildcat, the squabbling of coons, and the sudden flight of startled birds got on my nerves; the solid blackness outside of the tiny searchlight was peopled with strange wild creatures, and when a frightened frog splashed in the water beside us, the circle of light from my lantern flashed to the tree tops, and the captain behind me chuckled. I asked him in a whisper if he had seen any alligators.

"Plenty; the lake's full of 'em; just run over one," he replied, adding with gentle sarcasm, "'Gators don't climb trees."

For the next few minutes I took lessons in fire hunting and learned to recognize the dull red reflected gleam from the reptile's eye, and to judge of his size when both eyes showed, from their distance apart. I steadied the light on a pair of widely separated eyes that seemed to float far out from shore. As the skiff moved toward them, I could trace the outlines of the head and back of a large alligator floating on the surface. As I was lifting my rifle the captain whispered, "Not yet," and again, "Not yet," until, when at length I fired, I took no aim but held my weapon so near the creature's head that the powder must have burned

A captured alligator on the Lillie, around 1910.
Credit: Florida State Archives

him as the bullet smashed his skull. Since that night I have often fire hunted with a camera, but never with firearms.

A score of years ago the water in the Big Cypress country was filled with alligators, and it was not uncommon for fire hunters to take a thousand of the reptiles from a single small lake. I photographed a portion of a circular pond, one hundred yards in diameter, enclosed in a cypress strand, and the print showed seventy-three alligators floating or swimming upon the surface of the water. While exploring the country north of Cape Sable I camped one night with my guide on the border of a lake of mingled mud and water, stirred by small tarpon and other fish and reptiles to the consistency of porridge. The water that I ate failed to satisfy me, and the mosquitoes drove me early under my bar, hungry and thirsty. The step of a bear near our bars woke us up in the early evening, and we crawled out with our rifles in the light of a moon that was nearly full. We crawled back pretty quickly, my guide having stepped on a cactus and I having been attacked by a solid mass of mosquitoes, so savage that they frightened me. As I couldn't sleep, I asked my guide to tell me what he knew of the lake beside which we were camped.

"You know my old partner," said he, "Will Stevens, the feller that was shot at Naples; he went guidin' for you once? Well, him and me took 'leven hundred 'gators out o' that pond one year, and we skinned most on 'em on that little island you saw there. We packed pieces of dry-goods boxes from Low's place at the Cape and made a boat. I reckon I'll find it in the mornin'; 'tain't likely anybody's bothered with it. Pond was jest the way you see it now, garfish stickin' up their noses all over it, little tarpon rollin' and jumpin'; only the 'gators was thick, and when I first seed it I jest got behind a bush and grunted, and I'll bet I could hev walked clean to that island without steppin' off'n their backs. First off we didn't need a light to shoot 'em, but after we'd thinned 'em down a bit we used to shoot 'em at night, 'bout all we could skin next day. One day when we was skinnin' on the island, somehow the boat got away and drifted ashore. Will said he'd swim fer it providin' I'd stand by with the rifle and keep off the 'gators. Well, when he got 'most ashore I began to shoot all 'round him and hollered to him to swim fast, thet the 'gators was after him. He 'most busted hisself gittin' to shore, and I near died laffin'; but he jest walked off an' left me alone on thet island with a lot o' stinkin' carcasses till 'most night the nex' day. I ain't usually 'fraid o' 'gators, and would hev swum ashore, but this time they was too thick, and I reckon I must hev scared myself when I frightened

An uninvited luncheon guest, 1880s.
Credit: Florida State Archives

my partner."

Notwithstanding the great slaughter of alligators, the crop held out for many years, and as recently as 1898 the principal dealer on the west coast of Florida bought three or four hundred hides daily from about fifty hunters, and kept a schooner running to Key West with hides, and returning with cargoes of salt, ammunition, and grub. The price paid alligator hunters for hides varies from one dollar for those measuring seven feet or over, down to ten cents for such as measure less than four feet in length.

Fire hunting is so deadly that after a hunter has swept the surface of a river with his light it is scarcely worth while to look for alligators in that stream. The fire hunter has so nearly wiped out the saurian inhabitants of the rivers and lakes of the coast that their pursuit no longer affords him a living. Yet, whatever the work to which the hunter turns for support, he always stands guard against the return of the alligator. Last year I used to visit a colony of five alligators that I found at Clam Slough, on the west coast near Marco. One evening a Marco boy was told that 'gators had been seen at Clam Slough. "I'll go down to-night and git 'em," said he. I said nothing. My alligators were doomed. I could have saved them this time, but the next native who heard of them would have gathered them in. The boy sculled a heavy little canoe, that wouldn't safely hold two people, out of the big pass into the Gulf of Mexico on a moonless night, down the coast to Clam Slough, where he found and killed the five 'gators. He loaded his canoe to the gunwales with the carcasses, and I saw him at the Marco store the next day swapping five alligator hides for three dollars' worth of ammunition, tobacco, and grits.

The few remaining reptiles have been driven to their last refuge, their caves in the Big Cypress and the Everglades, where they are followed by a few hunters armed with iron rods, hooks, and axes, as neither rifle nor lantern is required in their work. In the dry season the water of the swamps and prairies recedes, leaving little shallow ponds and water holes dug by the alligators, from which they are hauled with hooks and knocked in the head by the hunters. These ponds and holes are filled with venomous snakes, and it is the belief of hunters that, as the alligators are killed off, the moccasins increase. Sometimes thirty or forty of these poisonous snakes can be seen about a single alligator cave. If the hunter happens to wear boots, he kicks the moccasins out of his way with the contempt which familiarity breeds. But even the hunter, when he hears the jarring of rattles, climbs a tree till he has located the king of snakes. Many hunters carry hypodermic syringes and permanganate of potassium, but few have faith in the drug as an antidote, and all have gruesome stories to tell of the effects of the venom secreted by the snakes.

The alligators killed at such hazard are skinned, the hides salted, and carried over bad trails and through swamps on the backs of hunters, and then poled in canoes many miles to the store of a trader, where they are sold for an average of less than seventy cents each. It is for this pittance, to a few of her citizens, that Florida permits the destruction of an attraction and an asset worth millions to the State.

The casual cruiser on the west coast of Florida, with the usual brass band methods, who explores a river in a day and explodes his way through its branches in another, will find the banks bare and the waters barren of alligators; but the camera man, possessed of the patience of the hunter and the persistence of the naturalist, may even yet obtain the saurian subjects his camera calls for. There are boys on the coast, born with much knowledge of the alligator and his ways, who will go out with him to the haunts of the reptile on the prairies and in the swamps, will follow a trail to a marshy pond, and coax a 'gator to the surface by grunting in his own tongue.

I have seen a barefoot boy, when the reptile refused to respond to his call, wade in the mud to his waist, explore with his toes till he felt the wiggle of the 'gator beneath them, then worry him to the surface, grab him by the nose before he could open his jaws, and tow the creature ashore to be photographed.

When an alligator that we were hunting crawled into his cave, I held a noosed rope over his mouth while the boy poked a stick through the mud until it hit the creature in his hiding place, and soon I had him snared, ready to be dragged out on the prairie and tied, to be kept till the camera man was ready for him. Then we turned the reptile loose on a bit of prairie, and the boy and I, armed with sticks, headed him off when he tried to escape, while the camera man, with his head in the hood of his instrument, followed the creature about seeking for evidence in the case of "Reason vs. Instinct." When the camera man was through with him, the alligator was set free, a final shot being taken at him as he walked off. Our hunter boys could never be made to comprehend our reasons for restoring to the creatures their freedom. They understood the photographing, but when this was done why not collect a dollar for the reptile's hide? Their manner implied that to this question no sane answer was possible. In the open waters of the rivers and the Everglades we used a tiny harpoon, stopped down so that it could only penetrate an inch beyond the barb and inflict but a trifling wound. We put little strain on the harpoon line, the purpose of which was to enable us to follow the creature until we could get a rope around his nose. Sometimes while paddling in a stream the odor of musk told of the presence of an alligator, and scrutiny of the bottom disclosed the reptile near, or under, the boat. Then a noose, made of the end of the painter, was slipped under the nose of the alligator, and after a brief struggle the creature was hauled aboard. After a few hours of captivity almost anything could be done with the reptile, although we were always shy of the unfettered jaws of a big one. Our hunter boy would stand in front of a large alligator and hold his mouth open for the camera man, but he was an exceedingly active youth, and never failed to jump a little quicker than the reptile. These alligators often played 'possum with us and allowed themselves to be tied in a skiff without a kick when we wished to tow them to some place convenient for the work of the camera man. But they were always on the lookout for a chance to make trouble; and once when we were quietly sailing down a river, towing a skiff in which we had tied a 'gator, the creature thought we had forgotten him, and breaking one of the lines which held him, bit a piece out of the skiff, capsized it, and rolled over and over with it in the water. We lowered our sails and worked frantically to straighten out the tangle before the reptile could drown. Meanwhile wind and tide swept us into the mangroves, which laid hold of spars and rigging and held us fast where myriads of mosquitoes assembled to drain us of our blood.

For the nature student the habits of the alligator hold much interest; to the camera sportsman he presents delightful possibilities; while to the every day tourist who will really seek him in his home he will give an assortment of sensations more thrilling than could be unearthed in a year of ordinary globe-trotting.

Hunt up the haunts of the creature until you find a river that he frequents. Paddle quietly and alone down the stream and up the creeks and branches that enter it, till you find on the bank the bed of an alligator with signs of his recent presence. Hide your skiff, sit down on the bed, and wait for him to come home. By and by, out in the middle of the stream, you may see three little black dots—the nose and eyes of your absentee landlord—and soon the whole head, tail, and back may appear. He will swim slowly toward you, and probably sink gradually beneath the surface before reaching the bank. If he comes on and crawls up on the bank beside you, it will be a high tribute to your coolness and complete control of your nerves, and the incident will make a pleasant place in your memory.

It happened once to me that after long waiting for the return of an alligator upon whose bed I was sitting, I discovered that he had not left it, but was lying in the tall grass just behind me, with his big jaws three feet from my face and his ten foot body curved partly around me.

After sitting silently in my skiff for half an hour, wondering why an alligator I had seen didn't show up, I chanced to look down and saw his head resting quietly on the surface of the water within twelve inches of my hand as it lay on the gunwale.

It gives a sensation to be remembered to sit thus, motionless, watching the unwinking eyes of this free, wild, powerful brute fixed gravely on your face, the huge jaws and the little that shows of the long white teeth within reach of your hand, and your hand within reach of jaws and teeth. Of course if you have the medieval instincts of some sportsmen, you may slowly, so slowly, reach for the weapon beside you and send a steel jacketed cylinder through the brute brain, and a couple of days later watch a bloated carcass floating high on its way to the Gulf, giving off an odor appropriate to the incident.

It is up to those of us who claim to be nature-lovers to look after the Florida alligator. We have just organized a society to weep at the bier of the bison—a creature which has been dead so long that he can be spoken of as was Lazarus—and have promoted clubs with number which pester Congress and the States to prevent by law the killing of game birds and beasts for food, that we may kill more of them for fun. We are working, almost without hope, for birds that are nearly extinct and animals which have been banished from their environments by the requirements of civilization, but we are neglecting a creature whose existence is imperilled, although his habitat is secure, his sustenance not threatened, and he only needs to be let alone to restore life and attractiveness to the waterways of a great national playground.

Alligators

by Marjorie Kinnan Rawlings

Here's a short story by one of Florida's best-known authors. Originally published in The Saturday Evening Post *(September 23, 1933), this tall tale—told in the Cracker dialect—is one that Rawlings heard during the years she lived at Cross Creek, Florida, hunting and fishing on the nearby lakes. While it does contain some elements that are considered racist today, we have kept the story intact to preserve the flavor of the narrator.*

B less Katy, I don't know nothing about alligators. You belong to talk to some of them real old-timey Florida 'gator hunters that has messed up with 'em deliberate. I don't never mess up with no alligator. If so chance me and one meets, it's just because he comes up with me—I don't never try to come up with him. There ain't never been but once when me and a alligator met more than accidental.

'Gators is a mess. And a pain. I run over one last night. I'd been out to Lobkirk's for a snort, and coming back by Gopher Creek I saw the knocker climbing out of the ditch to cross the road to water. I shot the juice to the Model-T and I hit him just the time he got his head over the rut. When he rared up, he carried the front wheels of the car plumb over in the ditch. The Model-T shook loose, but before it got shut of him, he had me going in the creek. I don't fancy 'em.

I don't much mind handling a small un. Partickler if it's to torment somebody is worse scairt of 'em than me. Like Br'er Cresey. He hates a varmint or a snake or a 'gator the most of any man I know. I don't never get my hands on a little alligator but I goes to studying: Where can I put him so's Br'er Cresey will get the most good of him? Cresey'll holler like a woman if you catch him just right. A while ago, me and Raymond caught him just right in the post office.

Br'er Cresey was standing back of the delivery window, sorting mail from the 2:10 train. We eases in at the back door and lays a three-foot 'gator just back of his heels and eases out again. Directly the 'gator goes to blowing. A 'gator's the blowingest thing I know of. 'Tain't rightly a blowing, nor yet a sighing, nor even a groaning—you know the way it sounds. It's a damn peculiar sound—partickler in a post office. Cresey looks around and sees nothing. Directly the 'gator heaves another. Cresey looks down between his legs and there's the alligator bopping his lips and blowing.

Now, Cresey come out from behind that delivery window like a man with ants in his breeches. He squealed and whinnied like a Maud mule, and when he sees me and Raymond, he goes to cussing. It's a pure treat to hear Br'er Cresey cussing. He calms down when we takes the 'gator off. He don't know we'd only moved it to the back of the express wagon. The rest ain't so funny. He was so mad, and scairt, too, when he steps on the 'gator in the express wagon, he just picks it up by the tail and pitches it. I happens to be the first thing in the way, and when Br'er Cresey pitches the alligator, bless Katy if it don't land on me and get all wropped around my neck. And I don't enjoy that much more'n Cresey.

When I was a young un, I fooled with alligators a little. I used to go with Rance Deese when he'd go hunting 'em. A little old shirt-tail boy, here I'd go barefooted across the flat-woods with Rance. You didn't never know there was alligators in the flat-woods? Why, sure, there's alligator caves there. Ain't you noticed there's always cypress ponds in a flat-woods? The 'gators travels in from the lakes and creeks to them and builds theirselves caves. Like a gopher hole, only bigger. They dig 'em in the pond bank, under the water. A 'gator cave's about three feet across and anywhere from six to fifteen feet deep, according to the 'gator's size and notions. He generally likes to holler it out so he can roll over in it. A 'gator's the very devil for rolling.

You take down around Fort McCoy in the pine. Look and you'll see a little piece of water. It'll lead off some way. You'll see in the mud where the 'gator comes up and suns hisself. In a dry time, them cypress ponds in the flat-woods goes dry, all excepting the 'gator caves. They're easy found. If you're aiming to catch the big 'gator, you take a hook on a pole and job it down. The 'gator'll bite it. You pull him out and kill him and skin him. 'Gator hides is worth about two-eighty-five right now for seven-foot or better. I've seen 'em go to four and a half.

The first time I come up with alligators personal-like was on one of them ja'nts with Rance Deese. Rance was grunting the little 'gators out of the caves. Calling 'em—grunting the way they grunt. Here they come, little 'gators, swarming to the top of the pond. Some of 'em comes out of the pond and goes to running ever' which-a-way. Rance was chooging 'em in a crocus sack. I was grabbing 'em here and yon. I had both hands full. I tried to get 'em all in one hand so I could grab and

Feeding time at the gator lagoon.
Credit: Florida State Archives

choog with t'other. Directly here one of them little scapers gets me by the finger and rips it clear open to the bone. I slung him here to yonder. He makes it up across the hill. I was eleven years old, but I had chitlin's enough to follow him and fall on him and catch him.

Rance hisself learned to be right respectful of alligators before he was done with 'em. I was with him one time at the Big Cypress slough—you know where 'tis. 'Gators like to get where there's a bunch of cypresses. They dig caves under the roots. Rance was kneeling down by a cave and fishing out little baby alligators about twelve inches long. He wasn't paying no mind, and directly the old mammy 'gator come to the top of the water and caught Rance across the neck with her tail like it was a cow whip.

You see, a alligator don't generally set out to bit you. He'll flip his tail toward his head, and whatever his tail brings in to him, he'll catch a-holt of. Rance ducked back out of range and the old 'gator sunk.

Rance jammed his hook down, but he couldn't find her. He said, "She'll turn up again."

He eased over into the water and went to wading. The water in the slough caught him just above the waist. There was little 'gators milling around in the water and he went on scooping 'em in. He'd stuff 'em in his shirt. Rance always wore his pants tight, and his shirt stayed down good, and when he waded in amongst 'em thataway, he'd get a shirt full before he come out.

Rance said, "Joog the hook down again, Freddy; see can you find the old un."

I jooged the hook down.

I said, "I can't find her, Rance."

He had his shirt full of little 'gators and he had both hands full.

He said, "I'll find her."

He wadded around some more, feeling with his foot. Now, I wouldn't say Rance found the alligator. It's more like it to say she found him. She heaved up out of the water, and before he could get out of the way she was right on top of him, flipping her tail. She smacked him square across the face with it, and next thing I knowed, Rance had lost his little alligators out of both his hands, and his footing to boot. The old mammy was right in behind him. He slipped and sprawled and made mighty poor headway, and I could see him changing his notions about alligators.

Just as he scrambled out, she caught the heel of his shoe in her teeth and commenced to drop back into the water. As soon as a 'gator catches anything, it'll go backward. Rance hollered to me to hand him something to bop her. I handed him a hatchet we had with us—had about a two-and-a-half-foot handle. Rance bopped her in the head with it—and you know that alligator let go of his heel and caught the handle of that hatchet in her mouth. Rance hated to lose the hatchet and he rassled with her. He finally got the hatchet, but he never got the alligator. Now, that learned Rance Deese to be right respectful of 'em. He kept that shoe with the heel bit for several years and he showed it to several people. That broke him from getting right in with a alligator. Now, me—I ain't never been unbroke.

You understand, it don't do to be too timid with a alligator. It just don't do. You got to know their ways, like them old 'gator hunters do, and you got to be bold according. If a 'gator faces you in close quarters, you got to watch your chance to shut his mouth for him, and when the chance comes, you got to take it or the 'gator'll take his. Like the night me and Raymond was gigging frogs in Black Sink Prairie. Raymond shined his light in a 'gator's eyes and shot him. He was about nine feet long and we dragged him in the boat. I was paddling the boat and Raymond was gigging in the bow. Now, it turned out Raymond had shot the alligator too far down the nose—not backwards to where his brains was. The 'gator wasn't dead—he was only addled.

I hollered to Raymond, "Shine your light back here!"

He shined his light back for me, and here was the 'gator with his mouth wide open. Right there is where a feller'd be in trouble if he was too timid. Raymond held the light steady. The minute the 'gator closed his mouth, I caught him by the lips and held them shut while Raymond finished him with a knife. You can hold a 'gator's lips together with one hand if you catch him with his mouth shut. But once he's got his jaws open, you can't get the purchase to close them again.

Alligators is mighty strong. They're that strong to where they can fool you. Like John Milliken at Salt Springs last week. We were gigging mullet. I seen a right small 'gator rise and sink. I whammed the gig into him. When I grabbed the gig handle he commenced a-rolling.

I says, "Here, John, hold him."

John takes the gig handle and says, "What is it?"

The 'gator was rolling to beat the devil. I like to fell in the spring, laughing.

I says, "Hold him, John—hold him."

The gig was purely playing a tune. It blistered John's hands and like to beat his brains out. How come it wabbling so, the 'gator had done grabbed the gig handle in his mouth. So, with him rolling, it made right hard holding. If a 'gator once shuts down on you, that's his trick—he goes to rolling. If he grabs your arm in the water, say, he goes to rolling. It's like to twist your arm right out of the shoulder.

Now, a 'gator will bite. Don't never let nobody tell you a alligator won't bite. I've knowed several fellers to get bit to hurt 'em. Nub-footed Turner—a twenty-foot 'gator bit his foot off. But generally speaking, a gator'll go his way if you'll go yours. But he don't like to be fooled up with. He most particklerly don't like nobody monkeying around his cave.

I remember one time there was three of us white men and a nigger working on the grove on the south side of Orange Lake. We knocked off for dinner and we goes in swimming, the way God made us. Gundy White, that was the nigger. Old Gundy.

The nigger says, "White men, what about lettin' me come in where you-all's at? Does you keer? If I was to go in and come out east a ways, I'd get powerful muddied."

'Twasn't muddy where we was. You know the current in Orange Lake is always going east.

We says, "You wait for us to come out."

So, when we comes out, Gundy goes in. He was just fixing to come out, about fifteen feet from shore. Bless Katy, if a big old alligator don't come up to him and catch him by the shoulder. Nothing serious—just turned him around and led him out about a hundred yards and turned him loose.

Gundy starts swimming back for shore, his eyes a-popping. He knowed good and well a 'gator'll pass up a dog any day to catch a nigger. The alligator swims back with him, head for head. When he gets to the same place, the 'gator catches him and leads him out again. He done it three-four times. It come to me we'd done been swimming over a 'gator cave. Three big white bodies was too much for the 'gator to bother. But let the one dark body go in alone, and the 'gator was man enough to turn him.

So I calls to Gundy, "Don't try to come out there! Come on out east a ways!"

He changes his course—and you know the alligator don't bother him a mite? Just sticks his head out and watches him. Just as good as to say, "You go do your landing somewheres else. You got you no business here."

That old nigger has 'gator sign on his shoulder to this day. It looks just like buckshot had tore out some little pieces.

We should of knowed we was over a cave by the smell. You remember the time me and you was fishing on Lochloosy and we couldn't find the bream on the bed? And we both smells something sweet and marshified? And I backs the boat up and says, "Wait a minute. It's a bream bed or a 'gator cave, one"? And we fished and fished and never did find no bream? It was a 'gator cave, sure. Ain't no mistaking it, unless it's bream. Peculiar—that's it. A 'gator cave just naturally smells peculiar.

I tell you who you belong to talk to about alligators, and that's Endy

Wilkers. He really knows 'em. He's still making a living 'gatoring and catching frog legs. He'd rather 'gator hunt than work. If 'twastn't for the alligators and the bullfrogs, Endy and his family would of gone hungry several times. I was with Endy one time when a fifteen-foot 'gator took us to ride. Me and Endy was on the dock when we seen the 'gator yonder in the lake. He was so big he looked like a rowboat drifting. We jumped in my fishing launch and heads for him. That was Endy—take right out after 'em.

The 'gator sunk. Then he pops up over yonder. Then he sinks again. He done it three times and don't come up no more. Endy knows then he's on the bottom. Bottom there was about nine feet. Directly we sees a row of blubbers. That was the 'gator breathing. The blubbers stop, and Endy lets him have the harpoon. Ka-whow! Just back of his hind legs. Endy knowed right where to feel for him.

Then bless Katy, here we go across the lake. We played out all our rope. I starts up the engine. You know we couldn't catch up with him? That 'gator was going better'n twelve miles a hour. He had to be, to keep the harpoon rope taut with the engine going. I threw it in reverse. It didn't no more'n slow him down a little. That 'gator was just naturally carrying us off. Sometimes it looked like he didn't have no more'n three feet of tail in the water. The rest of him was scrambling along on top. I never heerd such a fuss. It sounded like fifteen oxen a-wallering in the water.

He finally headed for a tussock to get shut of whatever 'twas he had, and Endy got the chance to shoot him. Whooey! When I'm riding on the water, I want to know where I'm going and can I stop what's carrying me.

I don't know but what I'd rather be behind an alligator than in front of one, come to think of it. I've seen one outrun a horse through the palmettos and across a flat-woods. Like Uncle Breck. He'd of give a pretty to of been behind the alligator the time it run him. That was over in Gulf Hammock, not far from the Gulf of Mexico. Me and Uncle Breck was to a pond, shooting ducks. The ducks'd circle overhead and we'd shoot 'em so's they'd fall in the woods behind us, and us not have to wade in the pond amongst the alligators. I'll swear, I never seen so many alligators. I reckon there was three hundred heads in sight, all sticking up out of the water. 'Gators just ain't plentiful in Florida now, the way they was then in Gulf Hammock.

I was watching for ducks—shooting and watching. Directly I hears Uncle Breck say, "Oo-o-ee-e!" Then he says, kind of faintified, "Shoot him, Fred—shoot him!" I looks around. Now, what he'd done to him first—if he shot him or what—I don't know, but it was Uncle Breck and the alligator across the woods.

Chasing him? The alligator was really chasing Uncle Breck.

I reckon there's been men has travelled faster than Uncle Breck. I don't reckon there's ever been a man has tried to travel faster. I mean, he was selling out. The 'gator was this high off the ground. . . . They made a turn around a bay tree. They was coming mighty near straight to me.

Uncle Breck calls in a weak voice, "Shoot him, Fred—shoot him!"

The devil of it was, I couldn't shoot the alligator for shooting Uncle Breck.

Directly they hits a log two-three feet high. Uncle Breck jumps it—he hurdled fast and pretty—and the alligator has to take a minute to waddle over it. It didn't stop him—a 'gator'll go right over a five-foot fence—but he couldn't take it as fast as Uncle Breck. The 'gator slowing down for the log give me the first chance, what with laughing and not craving to shoot Uncle Breck, to get a shot at him. And then, bless Katy, Uncle Breck was fixing to tear me down for not shooting sooner!

You wouldn't think it, but a 'gator's the hardest thing there is to kill, to his size. That is, to kill so he's dead good. Must be because his brain's so small he ain't got the sense to know when he belongs to be dead. One fooled me thataway just a while back when I was out with Endy Wilkers, and him 'gator hunting. We was in Indian Prairie, and it about dry. Endy was working the marsh edge and catching little old bitty ones, and he steps in a 'gator cave. The old mammy takened out after him. I shot one time and I figured I'd killed her dead.

We got her over in the boat and sets out. And bless Katy, all of a sudden that pebble-hided knocker comes crawling up between my legs, a-bellering. Her tail was going bam-bam. I looked for her to crawl out of the boat and I was fixing to shoot the rest of her head off. She just kept that tail a-going and didn't make no move to crawl out, and I couldn't shoot for putting holes in the boat. There wasn't nothing for me to do but get down there and straddle her. I sets down on her, one hand back of the eyes, and I popped my knife where her head joins together. I must of hit it plumb, for she ain't moved since.

But that un died easy, compared to some. Now, take the one I caught in my seine—that 'gator was really hard to kill. It was the spring I had me a seine on Lake Lochloosy. I owned a four-hundred-and-fifty-yard seine and two hundred and eighty fish traps and a fish house.

Nub-footed Turner pulled the seine for me on shares. The same feller I told you about—a alligator had bit his foot off.

Now all I knowed about a seine at that time was, you put it in the water and drawed it together. I knowed it had a pocket, but that was all. I used to use it, nice moonlight nights, to catch me six-eight bream and fry 'em on shore.

One night me and Nub-footed Turner was at the fish house on Lochloosy. Oh, my, it was a fine night, just as still and pretty. It wasn't too cold, it wasn't too hot. It was just a fine, calm night in the spring of the year. The lake was as still as a glass candle.

Nub says, "I'd just naturally love to go fishing tonight."

I says, "I ain't never really pulled the net since I've owned it, but I'll pull one end of it."

We goes out in the launch and throws the seine, and we takes about two hundred pounds of bream on the first haul. Now, Nub-footed Turner liked to fish on the moon.

He says, "I'd love to make a moon haul. I'd love to pull this seine just at moonrise."

Didn't neither one of us happen to know the time of moonrise.

I says, "We just as good to go on shore and eat."

We goes on back to shore and lights us a oak fire and cooks fish and coffee. Nub-footed Turner, he lays down and goes to sleep. I sets a while watching the east for the moon to rise. I commenced getting cold. Our clothes were wet and I couldn't never sleep right in wet clothes. So I totes up logs and limbs and builds up a big fire. I dried first one side and then t'other. Directly I lays down by the fire and goes to sleep. Now and again I'd raise up and look out east. By then I didn't want to go fishing.

I says, "I hope the moon don't never rise."

I lays down and goes to sleep again. Directly I wakes up, and here the east was done turned red, the moon was half hour high, and day a-breaking.

"Wake up, Nub," I says. "Here 'tis daylight and the moon done rose."

He says, "We'll pull a haul regardless."

We sets out in the launch close to shore in shallow water.

I says, "You jump off; I'll hold the land stake."

We lays the seine.

Now, how come the alligator in the pocket, it was thisaway. When one of them fishermen made a haul he'd do it easy and a alligator'd swim out of the net and sell out through them cypress timbers. Them as knowed this partickler 'gators told me he'd of swum out if he'd had the chance. But I didn't know no better and we worked too fast for him. He didn't get off at the right place.

I ties up the haul, and when the time comes, here I am, pulling away. We had the fish, all right, but directly the net commenced a-banging.

I says, "Nub, I'm tearing all the webbing loose from the lead line. The net's hung up on a log."

He says, "Next time it hangs, leave me see it."

"All right. It's hung."

He looks.

"'Tain't nothing."

I says, "Listen, Nub, there's a alligator in this net."

He says, "Yeah, but he's a little one. He won't hurt you."

I says, "Are you sure he's a little one?"

I was inside the circle and I had to pull it my way. I had to hold fast on the lead line to keep from losing the fish. The circle got right small.

Directly Nub says, "Wait, Fred."

I says, "Nub, you ain't lied to me?"

Now, we'd done had a couple of snorts, but not enough to where I wanted to catch no alligator.

I says, "Nub, I'm as close to what's in that net as I aim to be. Now, if that 'gator catches you, don't never say a alligator caught you and I goed off and left you. I'm just telling you ahead of time—I'm gone now. I hate to leave you, but I'm gone."

He says, "Come back here with your pistol."

I says, "I'll come a foot closer."

I untied the launch from a cypress tree. I pulls up on the lead line. I shot the .38 where I figured the 'gator belonged to be.

Nub says, "You got him."

All right. I pulls up the seine. I knowed I'd killed him. You ever fished a seine? Well, you have to fish the pocket out. We fished out the pocket.

I says, "Where'd that alligator go?"

About that time something comes up between us.

I says, "Nub, the first man moves is the first man caught!"

That alligator's head was three feet long. He was bopping his lips, and when they was wide open you could of put a yardstick between 'em. His mouth come together. Nub catches his lips.

He says, "Gimme your pistol."

"Here 'tis."

Nub shot him in one eye, one ear and the neck. The 'gator lays quiet. We goes on fishing the net. Then we piled the net on board the boat. We like to turned it over, loading the alligator. We finally got him in, facing to the rear. He had his front legs laying on a seat. Nub, he climbs in the bow of the boat by the 'gator's tail. I got back in the stern on the pile of webbing, me and the 'gator face to face. I reloaded my pistol and picked up one of the twelve-foot oars and Nub takened the other.

Here we go, a-paddling. That alligator commences raising up on his toes on that seat.

I says, "Nub, I'm going to shoot him."

He says, "Fred, don't shoot him! You'll kill me. He'll settle down right where he is."

Sure enough, he did. He settled down. Then he begun winking that good eye at me. He raised up again that high to where I had to look up at him. He settles down and goes to winking. I ain't never objected to nothing much more'n that alligator setting there winking that red eye at me. I shot him in the good eye and in t'other ear, and that quieted him down for a little while. Directly he rared up and give a flounce. He hit that pile of webbing just about the time I left it. Now, if he'd hit where I'd done been, there'd of been no funeral—just a water burial.

We makes it on to shore. We had about three hundred pounds of fish. Nub takes a fish scoop and goes to shoveling fish.

I says, "Nub, never mind the fish. Let's get this alligator out of this boat."

When I said that, the daggone alligator rared up and knocked that fish scoop out of Nub's hands to where it ain't never been found.

Nub says, "Hand me another scoop."

About then the alligator takened a notion it was time to leave the boat. I want to tell you, the only way we kept him from going out was Nub lost his patience and takened a ax and chopped him through the backbone. He was thirteen feet and nine inches—and he was really hard to kill.

Now, that's just the way it's always been with me and alligators. I don't never mess up with 'em on purpose. No, no; the one time I fooled with one deliberate don't count. No use scarcely telling about it. 'Twasn't nothing in the world but the banana brandy. If 'twasn't for that, hell nor high water couldn't of got me to ride no alligator. And even

Large gators are difficult to handle in the water.
Credit: Florida State Archives

then, now mind you, even then I didn't, so to speak, figure on doing it. It was old man Crocky aimed to do it. Old man Crocky had done set the Fourth of July to catch the alligator that had been bothering people swimming at Lochloosy Station.

He was a big old 'gator, and by bothering, I mean that when people was swimming he'd come in close enough that they'd come out. Fourth of July used to be a big time at Lochloosy. I've seen five hundred niggers come down for the frolicking and fighting. The first train that come in would unload right peaceable. Then, as t'other trains come in, there was fights all ready, waiting for 'em. I was deputy sheriff at Lochloosy, but 'twasn't no use for one deputy to go in to 'em. It would of takened fifteen or twenty.

This partickler Fourth of July the word had done gone out that old man Crocky was fixing to ride the alligator out of Lake Lochloosy. What with the niggers swarming, and the white folks congregating, there was a crowd on shore like a Baptist baptizing. And you know, old man Crocky never did show up?

Now, I figured, long as there wasn't nothing one deputy could do to stop a crowd from quarrelling, I had the same right as them to enjoy myself on the Fourth of July. And the way I was enjoying myself was drinking banana brandy. You ain't never been high on banana brandy? There ain't nothing more I can say about banana brandy than this: It put me to where I got the idea it was my duty, as deputy sheriff, to take the place of old man Crocky and ride the alligator.

The word went out I was fixing to substitute for old man Crocky. Folks goes to clustering along the shore. I pushes in amongst 'em and I hollers, "Get out of the way! I'm fixing to ride the alligator!"

I remember somebody yelling, "You fixing to ride the alligator or is he fixing to ride you?"

And I can just remember me saying, "You go eat your rations and drink your 'shine, and leave me 'tend to the alligator."

I walks out into the water and goes to swimming. I have the stick in my fist old man Crocky had aimed to use and had left at the fish house. It was big around as my fist, and whittled to a point at both ends. I swims out a ways more. Directly here comes the alligator, starting in to meet me. He's got his jaws open. I swim up to him and feeds him the stick. I jobbed it straight up and down in his mouth to where he couldn't close it. The alligator commences rolling and I stayed on him, rolling too. Him with his mouth held open, it didn't pleasure him, rolling, no more than me. When he quits, I slings one leg over the back of his neck, and here we go, me riding the alligator.

I give him plenty of room. I knowed he wouldn't sink with me, for a 'gator's got sense, and he knowed he's drown hisself with his mouth open. I put my hands over his eyes so he couldn't see where he was going. I guided him thisaway and that just as good as if I'd been riding a halter-broke mule. The way I turned him, I'd job my thumb in one of his eyes. He'd swing t'other way to try and break his eye loose.

I can just remember, dimlike, the crowd a-cheering and the niggers screaming. I rode the daggone alligator out of the Lake Lochloosy and plumb up on shore.

You can see how come it to happen. 'Twasn't nothing in the world but the banana brandy. I didn't have no intention of riding no alligator. I ain't the man you belong to talk to at all. You go talk to some of them fellers that has hunted alligators. I just naturally don't know nothing about 'em.

Babe Ruth and the Alligator
by Kevin M. McCarthy

This true story is based on sections of Baseball in Florida *(Sarasota: Pineapple Press, 1996) by Kevin M. McCarthy.*

When Babe Ruth played baseball, first for the Boston Red Sox and then for the New York Yankees, he used to spend spring training in Florida with his fellow ballplayers. The publicity that he generated for the local town—whether Tampa, Jacksonville, Miami, or St. Petersburg—was usually positive and warmed the hearts of baseball fans in the cold North.

One particular experience in St. Petersburg, however, almost did Ruth in, as well as the positive image that the state had been engendering. When the New York Yankees opened up their spring training in St. Petersburg in 1925, they were to play at a new ballpark at Crescent Lake Field. Hopes were high that spring as they had won the American League pennant in 1921, 1922, and 1923, and had won the World Series in 1923. Ruth was expected to play a major role, as in fact he did.

On that first day of spring training, he made his way to the outfield, where he shagged balls and limbered up next to Crescent Lake. After a few minutes, however, he made a sudden beeline for the dugout, where Yankees manager Miller Huggins confronted him and asked why he had quit so suddenly.

"I ain't going out there anymore," Ruth responded. "There're alligators out there."

Sure enough, several gators had come out of the lake to see what was going on in the new ballpark. It took the embarrassed groundskeepers several anxious minutes to shoo the gators back into the lake.

Fortunately, the northern reporters did not blazon their headlines with "Gators Chase Ruth," but it was an embarrassing moment for the local chamber of commerce.

Ruth had one other experience with gators in Florida that annoyed him. In 1920, when he went with the Yankees to Miami to play an exhibition game, sportswriter Damon Runyon accompanied the team, sending back reports of the Yankees to New York newspapers. On that trip, Runyon bought a small alligator that he named Alice and that he seemed to prefer writing about instead of the team.

Ruth got so annoyed at being upstaged by Alice that he berated the writer with a barbed question. "Hey, Damon, who are you covering on this trip, me or an alligator?"

Runyon quickly responded, "I can't keep writing about your lousy home runs every day."

Only when Alice died in Washington, D.C., did Ruth return to Runyon's columns on a more regular basis.

Master of My Lake
by Jack Rudloe

The following true story, which appeared in Audubon *(July 1982), is by and about the man whom many consider the most important environmental writer of the Florida Panhandle. Jack Rudloe is the author of* The Living Dock at Panacea *(1977),* The Wilderness Coast *(1988),* The Sea Brings Forth *(1989), and* Search for the Great Turtle Mother *(1995).*

"MEGAN . . . COME, MEGAN . . . MEEGAAN!" My screams burst through the still morning air in desperation and disbelief. An enormous alligator had rounded the curve of the lakeshore and was bearing down on my Airedale. The cold, yellowish eyes, gliding just above the opaque water of Otter Lake, were fixed on Megan, my companion, my friend for the past three years.

Never had I seen a living creature move so fast, with such overtly grim determination. As the beast sped into the shallows, I could see the ugly white spikes of teeth protruding from its crooked, wavy jaws.

Megan was almost out of the water, swimming to me with a bewildered expression, unaware of the danger closing behind her in the lake where she swam almost every morning after a three-mile run with me.

Megan's feet hit the bottom.

She's going to escape.

I felt hope, joy. But the black, plated head put on a horrible burst of speed. More and more of the knobby, black body emerged from the eighteen inches of tannin brown water. There seemed to be no end to it.

"No! No! No!" I screamed and rushed forward, somehow hoping to frighten it away, but the reptile couldn't care less. Its attention was fixed on Megan with cold intensity. With an explosion of water, it lunged upward, rearing above my dog almost as tall as a man, its front webbed claws spread menacingly apart. Time seemed to freeze—it was if Tyrannosaurus rex had come to life.

Megan's confusion was transformed to terror. From somewhere inside the reptile came a hissing like a super-heated steam boiler. The hissing became a thunderous, unearthly roar as the alligator struck, clamping its tooth-studded jaws on my pet. Crashing back into the water, it twisted and rolled, driving her down into the mud and weeds.

It's killing Megan . . . My dog . . . My friend!

Something snapped in my brain. I have to do something—make it let go, intimidate the thing into forgetting its prey. Adrenalin surged through me. With a cry of rage, of fear, of instinct, I found myself running and leaping through the air onto the back of the thing attacking my dog.

* * *

Megan and I had been swimming at the lake for two years and had never been bothered by alligators. They were there sometimes, I knew. I had seen them—shy, wild alligators that sank out of sight when approached by humans.

Where this one had come from, or why it attacked, I didn't know. Perhaps it had been hanging around the boat ramp and picnic area on the far end of the lake where weekenders fed it fish heads until it became "tame" and lost all fear of man. But the water had been low, fishing was bad in the scorching July doldrums, and people stopped coming. The handouts dried up.

There was no telling how long the alligator had waited at the landing, a mile from its normal haunt. How many days had it watched us, its bulbous eyes raised just above the dark amber waters, not causing a ripple, measuring each of us against its growing hunger?

Otter Lake was one of my favorite places. Hidden away in north Florida's wilderness, it was a retreat from technology, telephones, doorbells, and monthly bills. When I got tired of sitting at the typewriter in the broiling hot summer, the cool waters of the two-hundred-acre lake always welcomed me and my dog. Towering cypresses with gnarled roots and fat buttresses rose high above the water, their tops lacy with green needles in summer, vivid orange after the first frost, and barren, skeletal, and silver-gray in winter. When it was too cold to swim, I came just to look at the great water oaks with their Spanish moss-draped branches and green resurrection ferns.

* * *

But now the dark water exploded and cascaded as the alligator slapped its tail. I slid over its plates and bumps, groping for a hold on its huge back. I felt numbing pain in my chest as my chin jammed into the ridged back.

My God! What a colossal beast! You're actually on the back of an enormous alligator! It must be ten, twelve feet long.

It was alien, bony to the touch, almost dry, not slimy. There wasn't an inch of give in that rigid, armored back. As I struggled with every bit of my muscle to throw it off Megan, it swelled with air, making the hard-plated scales that normally lay flat rise upward. The thing was suddenly bristling with bony spikes.

Ignoring me, the alligator surged forward and got an even better grip on Megan, who all but disappeared inside the horrid maw. My hands groped the soft underside of the monster's throat and felt the beaded leather and scales that are made into belts and purses. It was almost flabby.

The tail slapped again. Water exploded.

Keep clear of the tail, it can break your leg!

I was a puny, hairless ape trying bare-handedly to take on an armored, scaly dinosaur. Every inch of the brute was designed for survival and battle; the only weapon I possessed was a mouthful of ineffectual little teeth. No wonder our species invented sharpened stones!

I hung on, desperately clinging, and tried with all my strength to turn the murderous animal, to keep it from plunging into the sunless, deep waters.

I've got to force it up on land.

My hands groped along its back, and up to its mouth, right where its toothy smile hinged. At least here was a handle of sorts. But it was no more than a skull covered with leather. There was no flesh, no give.

I got a good grip, dug my knees into the sand, and yanked upward. The steel-trap jaws wouldn't yield. I sensed them shutting down harder, squeezing life and breath out of my Megan. I saw a flowing trail of bubbles.

If only I had a weapon. A knife!

She's drowning—I'm running out of time!

Again and again I dug in and pulled up on its upper jaw, but nothing I could do distracted it from its single awesome purpose. Fortunately for me, the saurian's only intent was to drag its prey down into the lake and drown it. Its small reptilian brain was able to focus on that and that alone. I was only a hindrance, not an alternative.

I felt my knees dragging through the weeds on the sandy bottom as the alligator pushed inexorably back into the water. I cursed myself for being out of shape from all the hours spent at the typewriter.

With all my might, I slammed my fist down between its eyes, again and again. The only result was pain in my hands. It was like pounding a fencepost. Time, depth, and distance worked against me as the alligator dragged Megan further out into the water. I was losing the territorial battle of terra firma versus the watery world.

The alligator is going to win. It's going to carry Megan into the depths and eat her. It's too strong. I'm going to lose. I won't lose!

Desperately I threw my one hundred seventy pounds into manhandling it, trying to turn it back into my world. For a second, hope returned. I succeeded. The beast did turn. But just for a moment. Then it lifted me up, swung around, and continued on its course.

The eyes . . . go for the eyes.

My fingers worked their way over the unyielding leather-clad skull. I found its eyes, but the two sets of eyelids, one membranous and the other a thick leathery cover, closed, automatically sealing off the alligator's only vulnerable spot. Tightly closed, they weren't soft and yielding. They felt like mechanical ball joints on a car. With all my might I jammed my thumbs down, but it was futile, as if I were jamming my thumbs against hard-rubber handballs.

All my eye-gouging succeeded in doing was making the alligator swim faster. Black water closed over my head; the bottom was now sloping off quickly, and the beast had water beneath it. Any advantage I had was gone. Now it was rapidly entering its own world, and for me it was no longer a battle of land versus water; it was one of oxygen versus the abyss.

I managed to force the alligator up and get my head up for one hard gulp of air before being pulled back down. Again I drove my thumbs into the brute's eyes. By now I knew that my efforts to save Megan were futile. Even if by some miracle I could free her, and she weren't already dead, how could she survive having had her bones crushed and lungs punctured by eighty-inch-long spiked teeth?

But I couldn't make myself let go. Again I tried to angle the alligator upward, directing its movement, using its own momentum the way you do when riding a sea turtle. But the water was too deep. And an alligator isn't a sea turtle. Its long tail swept back and forth, sculling it forward. I was towed rapidly out into the middle of the lake.

Once more I got the alligator to the surface long enough to grab another breath; and then we were going down again. Down into the lightless swamp water. I was exhausted, my lungs were bursting. No longer could I see any sign of Megan. My vision was limited to less than a foot—just enough to make out the alligator's coat of mail.

As the light disappeared I felt new fear. I would soon be out in the middle of the lake in twenty or thirty feet of water. The monster might slap me with its tail, drop Megan, and turn on me. The very fury of this primitive battle, the splashing, might draw and excite other hungry alligators. The fear closed over me—fear for myself.

I couldn't hold on any longer. Despairingly I let go and watched its plated trunk churning beneath me into the gloom. It went on and on and on, like a freight train. I saw the rear webbed feet, churning one after the other, and then the narrow, undulating tail with its pale underside flashing. I could not see Megan; I would never see her again.

I boiled up to the surface, erupted into the daylight, filling my lungs with air. When I could breathe again I let out the mindless despairing cry of a wounded animal. My arms and legs thrashed through the water as I headed toward the cypresses and beautiful oaks with their long twisted branches. Finally, hard sand grated beneath my knees; I scrabbled up on the shoreline, crying and yelling incoherently.

In horror, I turned and looked at the empty lake. It had swallowed up all signs of disturbance. Its calm waters mirrored blue sky, stacks of white puffy clouds, and moss-draped oaks. An osprey winged its way across the sky, calling its high-pitched chirp. It was as if nothing had happened.

I fled to my car, wanting to get out of there quickly, to leave it all behind me. I felt betrayed, assaulted, robbed. I sped over the sandy jeep trail, through the palmetto, bouncing over ruts and dips, scratching paint on scrub oak branches, until I spun out onto the highway and raced toward home, still screaming.

Why are you screaming? There's nothing you can do. Control yourself.

For days I remained shaken and depressed. I had fought with everything I had and lost. I missed Megan terribly. I kept seeing her golden shaggy face looking at me in bewilderment as I urged her out of the lake. Over and over again, in my mind's eye, that big black head closed in on her. Slowly, from the bruises and scratches and pains in my body, I reconstructed what had happened. The long linear scrapes on my chest had to have come from the alligator's dorsal bumps, the bruises on my ribs and belly were from its thrashing back and forth. The aches in my thighs were from straddling it with a scissor's grip.

"You sure loved your dog all right," my neighbor said incredulously, "but you didn't give a damn about old Jack! People have been hand-feeding that gator all summer until he about crawled up the boat ramp begging food. That's not the first dog he ate. Someone ought to call the game commission and have him shot before he grabs some young 'un.'"

I was glad to be alive. Jogging along the sandy roads alone, in the following days, I thought a lot about alligators. Fifteen years ago they were nowhere to be seen, hunted to the brink of extinction. Poachers roamed the swamps in small boats, catching those eerie red eyes in their light beam and blasting or clubbing away. Warehouses from Perry, Florida, and Waycross, Georgia, to Newark, New Jersey, were overflowing with illegally taken hides.

Then, in 1970, the U.S. Endangered Species Act banned the international sale of hides and alligator products. Florida passed a similar law, and the market dried up. Large-scale poaching stopped, and the alligator began to recover.

While alligators were increasing their numbers, the human population also swelled in Florida. As dredges sucked up the swamps and turned them into shopping centers and canals, the alligators were driven from their sawgrass and river-swamp homes. But they adapted, taking up residence in golf course ponds, marina basins, and canals. The Florida Game and Fresh Water Fish Commission has found gator nests in people's backyards and chased ten-footers out of carports. In the past ten years there have been three fatal attacks on humans and twenty-two maulings.

In 1978, Florida instituted the Nuisance Alligator Control Program. When someone complains that an aggressive alligator has moved into a backyard, canal, or lake, the state investigates.

If the reptile is deemed a threat, a licensed alligator hunter will be sent to kill it. The game commission auctions off the hides. The hunter, often an ex-poacher, is given 70 percent of the proceeds and is free to sell the tail meat—which tastes something like veal—to restaurants.

Not surprisingly, the game commission now regards alligators as a renewable resource, according to wildlife resources chief Thomas Goodwin.

In 1981, it again became legal to sell alligator products such as purses, belts, and shoes in Florida. State officials claim they can control the market by a complex system of tagging hides and packaging the meat, but the number of poaching violations has more than doubled since 1978.

Archie Carr of the University of Florida strenuously objects to the commercialization of alligators: "Once you open the marketplace and build up the demand for hides, you're dooming alligators and other rarer species of crocodiles to extinction. Overseas the demand for hides is insatiable. This just encourages the worldwide sale of other crocodilian species, most of which are nearly extinct." Then he added, "Aggressive alligators should be shot or carted off but not offered for sale. The state is using the few attacks on humans and the attacks on dogs as ammunition to open up wholesale commercial exploitation. We're going back to the 1940s when you could drive the whole Tamiami Trail and never see an alligator."

The problems of alligator protection are both complex and confusing, and I found myself torn. I couldn't stand the idea of seeing a reptile that has survived unchanged for the past sixty million years exterminated. They are the last of the dinosaurs. Paleontologists have unearthed six-foot-long skulls with six-inch teeth from crocodilians that may have measured forty-five feet long.

But the lake would never be the same for me. I shuddered when I thought that in the very spot where Megan was attacked we had taken our ten-month-old baby swimming.

Again and again I dreamed of the fight, only this time I had a sharp knife. I could stab it over and over into the alligator's corpulent belly and its throat. I could hurt it, make it feel pain. Ex-alligator poachers had told me about the spot in the back of its head where a single stab would kill it instantly, cutting through the spinal column. In my dreams I had a chance.

But those dreams were inconsistent with everything I had worked for. I had been involved in environmental causes for the past twenty years, trying to save blue herons, turtles, and alligators from man's technology, and perhaps in so doing to save ourselves. I knew the importance of these ancient beasts. Without them there would be an overabundance of less desirable fish, like garfish and bowfin, that feed on bass, crappie, and sunfish. Most important, during summer droughts, when swamps are parched and dry, gator holes often become the only source of water for everything from deer to wading birds. Without them the swamp would be a poorer place.

It was three weeks before I returned to Otter Lake and looked out over its placid waters. There was no sign of the alligator, so my wife and I launched our canoe. I wanted to see the alligator again, to begin healing the mental wound it had inflicted, to banish the nightmares. If possible I wanted to restore it to its proper place as a living, flesh-and-blood animal.

We were still close to the landing when suddenly there was an explosive splash: a swirl of water, and there it was—aggressive and brazen. It didn't sink out of sight as we approached but surged ahead away from our canoe, throwing a wake as it crossed our bow. For a moment the hatred and fear returned. I wanted nothing more than revenge—to blast that thing forever to kingdom come.

Before I rode that terrifying beast out into Otter Lake, as it clutched my dog in its jaws, I would have been able to view the whole thing objectively. But now I had been affected personally. Whether I would ever swim in that lake again I couldn't say.

Sitting in the canoe, I watched the new master of my lake move out into the middle and then slowly sink down into the depths. I was hot; the August sun burned down into my back. I wanted to swim in the cool water, but somehow I couldn't bring myself to do it.

The alligator surfaced again and looked at us boldly. It was just a matter of time. He was too bold. If not this year, then next year he would be destroyed as the nuisance alligator he had become. And when that happened—even though he had dragged me through hell and killed the dog I loved—it would be a tragedy.

Alligator Hunting in the 1990s
by John Moran

Photographer-writer John Moran describes how alligators made a remark-able comeback from near extinction and how the annual gator "harvest" keeps their numbers under control and less of a threat to the burgeoning Florida population.

I n the gloom of a moonless night, thick, motionless air envelops Tiny Cassels in his homemade wooden boat. He watches, and waits, ignoring the giant alligator tooth protruding through the splintered plywood floor. The enraged gator with the missing tooth is somewhere out there in the dark, sporting Tiny's harpoon tip in his back. When the gator explodes to the surface for another bite of his boat, Tiny is ready for him, finishing him off with a .357 magnum bang stick to the head, grateful no doubt that there is one less alligator alive in Newnan's Lake.

Rebounding from their spot on the first federal endangered species list in 1967, alligators are back. And so is alligator hunting. Before it was banned in 1962, the hunting of alligators in Florida had contributed to an alarming decline in their population during a century or more of commercial exploitation.

But with a soaring population of alligators pegged at a million or more, and thousands of nuisance alligator complaints annually, the Florida Game and Fresh Water Fish Commission (GFC) instituted a tightly regulated public waters alligator harvest program in 1988.

"The impetus behind restoring the hunt was to increase the commercial value of alligators, and in doing so, to increase the value of their habitat. The byproduct of that is preserving habitat for all wetlands species," said GFC alligator research biologist Woody Woodward.

The program follows seven years of experimental harvests on Orange, Lochloosa, and Newnan's Lakes in Alachua County in which researchers at the GFC wildlife research lab in Gainesville gathered data to determine the ability of a wild alligator population to withstand an annual harvest on a sustained-yield basis.

For the hunters, of course, the value of alligators is found not in data, but in dollars and, for some, recreation. In 1997, the month-long hunt gave 728 permitted hunters the opportunity to take five alligators each in 39 public lakes and rivers throughout the state. Selected by lottery from a pool of 14,000 applicants, the hunters must buy an alligator-trapping license—$250 for Florida residents, $1000 for nonresidents.

Though alligators can grow up to fourteen feet, the average length of a gator taken in the hunt during recent years is seven to eight feet. The average weight is 100 to 150 pounds, with about a thirty per cent meat yield selling for $5-6 a pound. Hides are cleaned, salted and rolled, then sold for about $20 a foot for the production of shoes, belts, luggage, and billfolds.

The Animal Rights Foundation of Florida has urged the cancellation of the annual hunt, calling it "barbaric" and "blatantly inhumane." The foundation argued in a letter to Governor Lawton Chiles that allowing hunters to kill a once-endangered species would "foster . . . disregard for laws protecting other endangered species."

Chiles defended the hunt in a written response to the group, saying it benefits alligators by attaching a commercial value to them.

In contrast to the well-attended protests of the early years of the experimental harvest, Elizabeth Howard of People for the Ethical Treatment of Animals was the only placard-carrying protester in sight on the first night of the annual hunt on Orange Lake. "People aren't real sympathetic," she said. "Gators are big and mean. I know people whose dogs have been killed by alligators." Even so, she said, "It's up to us to learn to coexist with the alligator."

Coexistence with alligators is a subject of increasing concern to the residents of a state whose population swells daily by almost a thousand. More people in Florida means less habitat for alligators, a fact not lost on the families of the nine people who have died in alligator attacks since 1973.

As more alligators show up in the backyards, swimming pools, golf courses, and drainage canals of Florida, public sentiment may side with the hunters. Attracted by the allure of a man-against-beast mindset, many of the hunters are new to the sport. For some, however, alligator hunting is a family tradition.

"I didn't have no choice; I had to learn how to hunt gators," said Danny White of Lochloosa, in rural Alachua County. "My daddy took me out on the lake one night. He took my gas tank and gave me a paddle and said, 'Don't come home till you got one'."

"Actually," he went on, "my momma taught me all I know about gator hunting."

"That's why he didn't catch none last night," quipped Danny's wife, Diane.

Such joking comes easily in this tight-knit family as they work together in their cramped alligator-skinning shed, a few hundred yards from the lake that provides not just a living, but a sense of history as well.

"I've been around gator hunting all of my life," said Columbus White, a state-licensed nuisance gator trapper for many years. "My daddy was a big gator hunter and my daddy-in-law had been hunting gators since before World War I. Those old gators paid for many a meal on our table," he said.

It's apparent now that Florida's alligator population is a long way from extinction. Florida's old-time alligator hunters—men like Columbus White—are a part of the state's cracker history that, unlike the species they hunt, may not survive forever.

Despite holding the state record with a monstrous 1043-pound gator he bagged on Orange Lake in 1989, Columbus discounts the notion that alligator hunting is a scary way to make a living. The hazards are obvious, he admits. But the only time he's concerned is when he gets in a tight place on the lake competing for space with other hunters. "If that gator makes a move, he's gonna run over someone," he said.

White and other hunters don't understand the outcry over their making a living on the sale of alligator meat and hides. For them, alligators are another of nature's offerings, akin to fish, turtles and frogs, which also supplement their income.

Does Columbus's wife, Mertie, worry about her man hunting gators on the lake at night? "Nah, I go to bed and go to sleep," she confides.

Evening is fast approaching when wildlife officers signal the start of the hunt, and hunters race away from the boat ramp on Newnan's Lake near Gainesville to claim their locations for a night of gator hunting.

(Opposite)

"It's very intense. You're constantly looking for their eyes," says Eddie Kadlec. With helmet-mounted spotlights, the hunters scan the surface of the murky lake, searching for pairs of alligator eyes reflecting like glowing embers. "The enjoyment comes from shining one down and harpooning it," he says. Embedded in the back of the alligator, the harpoon tip is attached to a float with a length of rope. The wounded alligator will thrash and swim until fatigued, enabling the hunter to follow the moving float and maneuver his boat close enough to finish the job.

(Above)

Death comes quickly to an exhausted alligator beneath the hyacinths of Orange Lake as Bobby Bass pumps a .357 Magnum shell into its head with a bang stick. Columbus White, Bobby's father-in-law, looks on. It was their second kill of the night; the first reposes in the back of the boat.

Harmless in death, a Newnan's Lake gator joins Columbus and Bobby for the boat ride to shore.

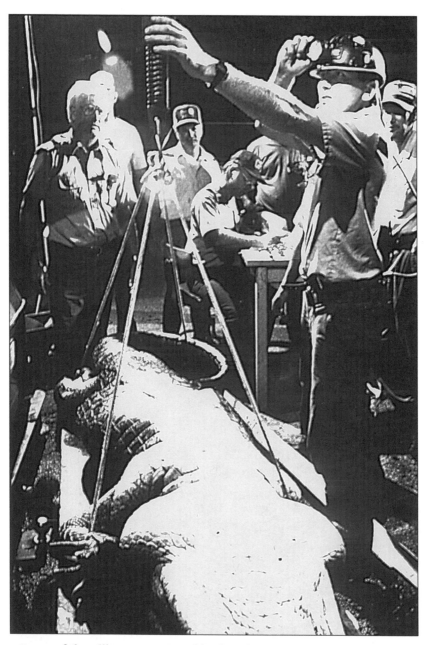

Some of the alligators were so big that the winch used to weigh them buckled and had to be replaced. Game and Fresh Water Fish Commission biologist Woody Woodward takes a reading on a 600-pounder killed in Orange Lake. As the hunters returned to shore about midnight with their night's kill, curious onlookers appeared.

"For us, it's a form of sport, a challenge. We enjoy it. If we didn't like it, we wouldn't be doing it," says Bobby Gibson, standing behind his brother Barry in their custom alligator cooler in Marion County with their haul from several nights of hunting on area lakes.

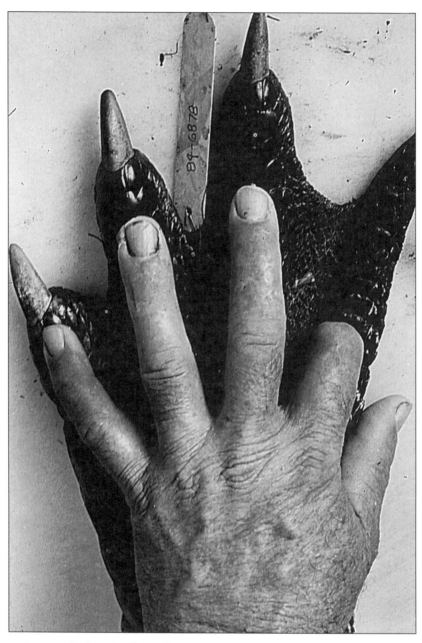

Contemplating the finger he lost to a hungry gator, Columbus White recalls with wry understatement, "I thought that alligator was dead. But he wasn't." An alligator control agent for the state, Columbus was working a nuisance gator call on State Road 20 when the incident occurred in 1981.

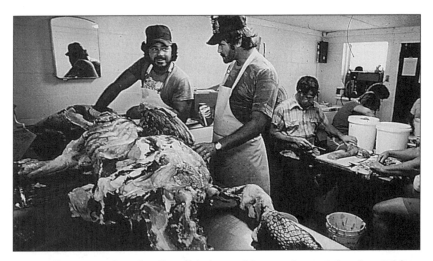

Skinning gators is a family affair in Lochloosa where Columbus White (rear background), his wife, daughter, son, daughter-in-law, son-in-law, and a family friend all pitch in with the day-long task of cleaning a 645-pound alligator, the third largest he's ever caught. "It was so big, we had to signal another hunter to help me and Bobby load it in the boat. And we already had a 400-pounder in the boat," Columbus says.

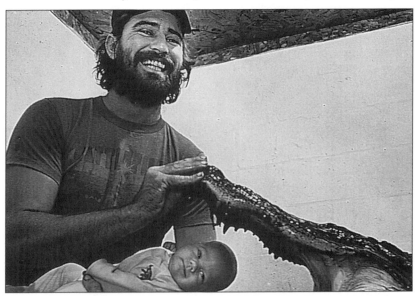

Boss Cassels jokingly offers up his seven-week-old daughter, Jessica Renae, as gator bait. Seeming a little unsure about Boss's sense of humor, his wife, Teresa, says, "I guess it's OK seein' how the gator is dead."

Walk on the Wild Side:
Biologist Kent Vliet Gets
Close and Personal with Gators

by Cathy Dillon

Perhaps no other human being has willingly swum so close and so often with alligators as Kent Vliet, who has spent his career studying the animals. This story was originally published in University of Florida Today *(June 1989, pp. 22–26; reprinted with permission of the publisher).*

Kent Vliet never keeps alligators at arm's length—although once he wished he had. He was riding on the back of a gator trying to lasso the reptile when it plunged into a depression in the murky lake at the St. Augustine Alligator Farm. It slipped beneath the belly of another large alligator, which became so angry it lunged for Vliet and rammed its jaw on his arm.

The gator punched a tooth into Vliet's flesh. Had it bitten down, the creature could have dragged Vliet to the bottom of the lake, mutilated his arm, gone into a death spin, and killed him.

The next weekend Vliet was back at the lake climbing on top of alligators as dozens more warily watched nearby.

"I've never really let those animals bother me too much," Vliet says offhandedly. "I think a lot of the fear people have about gators comes from not knowing them well."

Vliet knows alligators well, having waded in gator-infested waters for nearly a decade to observe the reptiles eyeball to eyeball. The adventures of the 32-year-old University of Florida biology instructor have been dramatized in a National Geographic documentary, chronicled in *The New Yorker* and *Time* magazines, and featured on television's *PM Magazine* and *The Today Show*.

People have a primeval fascination with alligators, whose sixty-foot ancestors appeared with dinosaurs during the Mesozoic Era about 230 million years ago. "Staring out over a Florida swamp or lake today and seeing a reptile that resembles a dinosaur is almost like looking back in time when reptiles were large and dominated the world," Vliet says.

Terror at the thought of being injured or killed by a wild animal also explains human curiosity about alligators, sharks, tigers, bears, and other toothy predators.

"I'm so relaxed with gators that I often take too many chances and work too closely with them," says Vliet, a man whose stocky, muscular build belies a laconic, easygoing manner.

"And I put myself in a position where, if they really wanted to, they could cause me a lot of trouble."

Tourists at the St. Augustine Alligator Farm morbidly joke as Vliet wrestles alligators in the water with his bare hands. "Well, I see you still have two legs and they're both the same length," says one man as Vliet climbs out of the lake. Vliet smiles. "Yeah," he says, "but I used to be a lot taller."

Lizards—not alligators—intrigued Vliet when he entered UF's graduate school in 1980. As a boy growing up in central Oklahoma, Vliet caught a rich variety of snakes and lizards that roamed the rolling hills, grasslands, and riverbanks around his hometown of Norman.

With alligators so abundant in Florida, Vliet decided to study their surprisingly mellow courtship at the alligator farm.

"Courtship in alligators is a slow, languid process of pairs of animals coming together and nudging, pushing and pressing along the face, head and neck of one another," he says. "We think of alligators as really big and tough creatures, but they can be very gentle in their sexual interactions."

As the love affair intensifies, gators will try to force each other underwater as a test of strength. "That's an important aspect of an alligator's decision whether or not to continue courtship and actually go ahead and mate," he says.

Like other large reptiles, the alligator male must show the female that he can restrain her before she becomes receptive to mating. These bumps and pushes may even stimulate the production of the right reproductive hormones in the female, Vliet says.

Alligators hadn't been bothered much when Vliet began tagging them at the farm for his first courtship study eight years ago. The creatures, with their guard down, were easy to lasso from the boardwalk and pull ashore.

But one gator was alert.

Vliet and his partner got into a boat and went after the reptile,

These Seminoles made a living wrestling alligators.
Credit: Florida State Archives

which at ten-and-a-half feet and about 500 pounds was the largest in the lake.

"As soon as we slipped the rope over its head, it took us for a real sleigh ride, dragging us all over the lake with little to do but hold on to the side of the boat," he says.

Vliet grabbed the boardwalk as the boat passed by and hung on desperately until his helpers were able to grab and rope and release the gator.

"I still remember that one day when we got pulled all over the lake by number 31," he says.

Although Vliet numbers the gators he is studying, he has come to know and even name some of them by their broken teeth, unusual bumps, and other distinguishing marks. There is "Leaping Larry," a real nightmare of a gator who springs without provocation; "Pirate," one with a white eye; "Texas Jack," named for its home state; and "Old Blue Eyes," whose name speaks for itself.

Alligators have a brain the size of a walnut, but are pretty smart in sizing up their environment. They can distinguish Vliet's footsteps from the sounds of a gator and know the feel of the rope he uses—backing out of it before he can tighten the noose.

Once the gators knew his tricks, Vliet had to get into the water to catch them.

He donned a diving mask and snorkel and inched into harm's way, only to have a gator about 60 feet away turn and charge.

Vliet quickly stood up. He hoped his height would intimidate the alligator. The gator stopped only a few feet away. Both froze for about 10 seconds. Then Vliet splashed water in the gator's face and scared it off.

"They aren't terribly aggressive animals like people think they are," Vliet says. "Only in the hottest part of summer and only the biggest males are willing to really come at you. And even then they will only have courage for one attack."

Alligators are most aggressive during their active summer months. Cold-blooded creatures that don't generate energy to maintain body heat, alligators stop eating and are slothful from December until late March.

Nesting females probably are the most dangerous threat to humans, but chances of an attack are rare since the nests are usually concealed in dense underbrush.

In Florida, alligators have killed five people and bitten an average of six to eight each year since records were kept in 1972. State wildlife officials think there could be as many as a million alligators in Florida.

Vliet believes confrontations between gators and humans are likely to increase as the state's human population continues to boom. Newcomers build houses near lakes, rivers and ponds where alligators live, and many are frightened Northerners with little tolerance for the reptiles, he says.

"People must learn how to live with alligators if they want to reduce their chances of accidents," he says.

As humans invade their territory, gators may become "nuisances" by appearing in swimming pools and backyards or eating dogs and cats. People can have these alligators removed and killed as part of the state's nuisance alligator program, resulting in about 4,500 deaths in 1988 alone.

Humans who feed alligators are to blame for some of the attacks, Vliet says. With the demise of great predators, Americans have lost their fear of wildlife, throwing marshmallows to bears in Yellowstone National Park and to alligators in Florida.

"Never feed an alligator," Vliet says. "It may be fun to watch and it may be fun to impress your friends, but it's definitely bad for the alligator."

Alligators then lose their natural fear of people and often bite the

---

Alligator Tales

hand that feeds them. Other attacks on humans are largely misidentifications, in which an alligator, for example, mistakes a swimmer's bobbing head for that of a small animal.

Vliet knew he had to meet the gators at water level because he observed from the safety of the boardwalk that the reptiles used body posture and weight to communicate with each other. He fantasized about swimming into the lake with a fake alligator and courting a real reptile.

Using a long pole, Vliet waded in and maneuvered "Syngator," his name for a dead alligator skull that had been painted and filled with foam to resemble a living creature. "Alligators would court it for a minute or two, but then they would either swim away or physically attack the thing," he shrugs. "It probably didn't smell like a real alligator."

These days, Vliet swims with gators to get blood samples for a study on whether crowding causes stress and reduces their production of sex hormones. He believes captive alligators aren't likely to find love in a crowded swamp.

Vliet, who was featured in the 1985 National Geographic documentary "Realm of the Alligators," may not study the reptiles forever.

"I take so many chances with alligators that sooner or later I'm going to get hurt pretty bad—lose my arm or something—and I probably wouldn't be able to work well," he says.

Besides, Vliet has an interest in many critters, including snakes, bats, and vultures.

If he couldn't work with alligators and had to pick another creature to study, what would he choose?

"Sharks," he says. "I've always been fascinated by them, and they're even less understood than alligators."

Gators: An Uncuddly Bestseller

by Gary Kirkland

Marketing the gator: what a concept! This story originally appeared in The Gainesville Sun *("Business Monday," October 14, 1991, pp. 8, 11; reprinted with permission of the newspaper).*

Silently sliding through the cattails and cypress knees, its eyes flare like coals from hell as the flashlight beam sweeps the inky surface of the water.

With jaws strong enough to crush a man's skull, its body encased in armorlike hide, the ten-foot alligator is a survivor of the dinosaur age, a presence that both inspires and terrifies.

As long as folks have walked the sandy soils of the peninsula, somebody's figured a way to make a buck off the creature the Spanish dubbed "el lagarto" or the lizard. Sure, the hides make great shoes, bags and belts and the meat is a delicacy, but it took a true marketing visionary to see 600 pounds of thrashing muscles and teeth as the perfect shape for a napkin holder or back scratcher.

It could hardly be voted most likely to succeed. It's not close to cute, it's not fuzzy and has never been considered cuddly. Turning a rodent into a Disney movie star is one thing. Getting people to embrace a cold-blooded meat-eating reptile has taken one heck of a sales pitch.

"Sure, it's got lots of teeth and can swallow poodles like Vienna sausages, but that long shape is perfect for a doorstop," one of Ponce de Leon's tourist development officers may have reported. "Forget this Fountain of Youth stuff; just picture one of these rascals in glazed ceramic with its mouth open. You've got an ashtray. Why, the smoke can even roll from the nostrils. We'll make a million and forget about finding the City of Gold."

By the time Florida reached statehood in 1845, there was speculation that a little-known clause in the documents signed by President James K. Polk set a requirement that one in three souvenirs leaving the state carry an alligator likeness.

He may even have celebrated the event at a posh state dinner where he seasoned his feast with gator motif salt and pepper shakers.

From simple beginnings, it was only a matter of time before alligators migrated to tea cups, shot glasses, toenail clippers, bottle openers, thermometers, road maps, collector spoons and thimbles.

The most mundane items could bask in the aura of sunshine and radiate the adventure of the tropics by the addition of a few skillfully applied dabs of green and black enamel.

Perhaps the biggest advancement in gatornomics came when some unknown artists advanced the reptilian evolutionary clock. Suddenly, creatures that for millions of years were content to slither, crawl or swim were now walking on two legs.

The University of Florida went a step further, concluding an animal with a million-dollar hide surely needed a set of clothes to be decent. So The Gator, complete with letter sweater and freshman beanie, waddled into the market. For formal affairs, a top hat, tails and cane became the standard attire.

Even though UF's Albert has been domesticated, he still maintains a fierce demeanor. But by dropping the teeth and adding a goofy voice, the king of the swamp was swimming into Saturday morning cartoons. With big blue eyes and a saddle, a plastic version of Florida's official state reptile prowls the malls as a kiddie ride, 50 cents for 30 thrill-packed seconds of bouncing.

It's also an idea too good to keep cooped up inside the confines of the Sunshine State. In Meadville, Pa., 90 miles north of Pittsburgh, 90 miles east of Cleveland and 90 miles southwest of Buffalo, is Allegheny College. The alma mater of President William McKinley, Allegheny is the 32nd oldest college in the country and home to the NCAA 1990 Division III football champions, the Gators.

IV. Native American Folktales About the Alligator

Native Americans believe that every animal has a mind and a will and should be treated with respect, and they tell stories and folktales about many different animals. They use such tales to teach their children how people and animals can live in peace and help each other. The alligator plays a role in some of these stories.

The first three tales are based on John R. Swanton's *Myths and Tales of the Southeastern Indians* (Norman: University of Oklahoma Press, 1995, pp. 51, 52, 22). The fourth tale is based on *Native American Legends*, compiled and edited by George E. Lankford (Little Rock: August House Publishers, 1987, p. 122).

Why the Snake and the Alligator Are Friends

(from Myths and Tales of the Southeastern Indians *by John R. Swanton)*

One time Mr. Rabbit decided to try to get two pond creatures—the snake and the alligator—to become enemies. If the two enemies killed each other, then Mr. Rabbit would be able to use the pond without worrying about being hurt by either animal.

One day Rabbit went to a pond and saw Mr. Snake. He said to the snake, "Mr. Alligator wants to hurt you."

Mr. Snake answered, "Just let him try. I am fast enough to attack him."

Then Rabbit went to find Alligator and told him, "Mr. Snake wants to hurt you."

Alligator said, "Just let him try it. I am big and strong enough to kill him."

Rabbit then got the two animals to have a tug-of-war, using a vine between them to see which of the two animals was stronger. Snake took hold of one end of the vine, and Alligator took hold of the other end. They began pulling and pulling just as hard as they could, but neither one could win the tug-of-war.

They finally decided to call the tug-of-war a draw and not say anymore that one was stronger than the other. In fact, they became friends. And that's why they have ever since then been able to swim in the same water, whether pond or stream or river, and not hurt each other.

How Rabbit Fooled Alligator
(from **Myths and Tales of the Southeastern Indians** *by John R. Swanton*)

One day Rabbit saw Alligator sunning himself on a log. Rabbit went up to him and asked, "Alligator, did you ever see the devil?"

"No, Rabbit, I never did. But if I did, I wouldn't be afraid of him."

Rabbit said, "Well, I saw the devil a short time ago, and he told me that you were afraid of him."

"Nonsense," said Alligator. "If you see Mr. Devil again, tell him that I'm not afraid of him one little bit."

"If that's true," said Rabbit, "come up to the field tomorrow morning and I'll show you Devil. And if you see any smoke in the field, don't worry. That's just Mr. Devil coming over the field."

"OK," said Alligator, "I'll be there."

"And if you see any birds and deer rushing out of the field, don't worry and don't be afraid."

"Don't worry about me, Rabbit. I won't be afraid."

"And, Alligator, if you feel the grass burning and getting hot around you, don't worry. That just means that Mr. Devil is getting close, and you'll be able to get a good look at him."

"OK," said Alligator.

The next morning, Alligator kept his word and made his way slowly into the field. Rabbit had him go to the center of the field, far away from the river, and take his place to wait for Mr. Devil.

When Rabbit saw Alligator so far from the river, he had to laugh to himself and think how clever he was. Then he ran off to a campfire and got a little torch to burn and took it back near to where Alligator was. Rabbit then touched the burning torch to the dry grass, and it began to burn.

When the birds and deer rushed out of the burning field, Alligator shouted to Rabbit and asked why the field was burning.

Rabbit said, "Don't worry, Alligator. That just means that Mr. Devil is getting close. It won't be long now before you get to see him."

"OK," said Alligator, "but it sure is getting hot."

Alligator wrestling in the 1960s.
Credit: Florida State Archives

Pretty soon, the fire was burning hot, and the smoke was getting thick.

"What's going on, Rabbit?"

"Don't worry, Alligator. That's just the Devil's breath. He'll be here soon."

Then the flames got closer and closer and began to burn Alligator's stomach. He rolled over and over to try to put out the terrible pain on his stomach, but that only made it worse as the flames got hotter.

"Don't move so much, Alligator," Rabbit shouted. "You need to lie still to be able to see Devil."

But Alligator couldn't stand it any longer and ran off as fast as he could across the burning field into the river. When he saw Rabbit rolling on his back and laughing at him, Alligator knew that he had been tricked.

"I thought you weren't afraid of Devil," said Rabbit, as he continued laughing at how he had tricked Alligator.

From that day on, Alligator did not believe anything that Rabbit told him.

How the Alligator's Nose Got Broken

(from Myths and Tales of the Southeastern Indians *by John R. Swanton*)

If you look closely at an alligator, you may notice that right behind his nostrils is a little dip. Well, that dip comes from the fact that many years ago the gator got his nose broken by the eagle. It all happened in a ball game that all the animals of the forest were playing.

The alligator was the leader of all the four-footed animals. They challenged the birds to a ball game. The leader of the birds was the eagle. On the given day all the animals showed up, with the alligator and his four-footed friends on one side and the eagle and his bird friends on the other side. The referee put two poles into the ground at each end of the field. The poles were about ten feet from each other. The idea was for each side, the four-footed animals and the birds, to throw a ball between the poles at the opposite end of the field.

The referee signaled the sides to begin the game by tossing a ball on the ground between the four-footed animals and the birds. The alligator caught the ball right away, put it between his teeth, and ran to the other end of the field to try to throw it between the two poles that the birds were guarding.

The birds flew all around him, trying to distract him so that he would drop the ball. All the four-footed animals were cheering on the alligator and hoping that he would get to the poles and toss the ball between them. The birds got discouraged at not being able to get the ball away from the alligator, but the eagle thought of a way to win the game. Just as the alligator got to the poles and was about to win the game by tossing the ball between them, the eagle flew high into the air and then shot down like an arrow until he struck the alligator on the nose and broke it.

The alligator was in such pain that he opened his mouth to yell. At that point, the turkey quickly poked his head into the mouth of the alligator and pulled the ball out of the alligator's teeth. The turkey then ran to the other end of the field and threw the ball between the poles and won the game.

Ever since that time, the alligator has had a broken nose or at least what seems to be a broken part of his long snout.

How an Alligator Helped a Hunter
*(from **Native American Legends**, compiled and edited by George E. Lankford)*

One particular Indian village had a lot of good hunters. In fact, except for one unlucky man, all of the hunters were very skilled at finding deer, killing them, and providing the village with venison.

The one man who simply could not shoot his arrow fast enough to kill the deer was very discouraged. He was quiet enough to find and creep up on the deer, but whenever he got ready to shoot his arrows, the deer heard him and ran off.

Once, after he had been away from his village for three days and had not succeeded in killing a single deer, he saw an alligator lying in the middle of a field. The gator had also had a streak of bad luck and had not been able to find any water to drink in days. He was becoming so dry and thirsty that he could barely speak.

He might usually be afraid of a hunter, but this gator was so close to death that he was not at all afraid of the man. Instead of trying to run away, the gator waited for the man to come close and then asked if he knew where any water was in the area. The hunter responded, "Over in that forest is a deep pool full of clear, refreshing water."

"I'm too weak to travel over there by myself," the alligator moaned. "I need help to get there. Please come closer so we can talk. I won't hurt you. I'm too weak from thirst to attack you."

The hunter worked up his courage and went closer to the alligator. "I know you are a hunter," said the gator, "who has not had much luck in killing deer. The other Indians are very clever at finding and killing deer for their village, but you have not been successful. If you carry me to the water over in that forest, I will tell you how to kill as many deer as you find."

The hunter wanted to help the alligator, especially if the animal could help him kill deer, but he was afraid of the reptile. So he said, "I'll carry you, but only if you let me tie your legs together and tie your

---

156

mouth shut so that you won't be able to hurt me."

The alligator agreed. "Go ahead and tie my legs together and tie my mouth shut. I'm too weak anyway."

And that's exactly what the hunter did. After tying up the legs and mouth of the alligator, the hunter lifted him up and carried him over to the forest, where he untied the gator and put him into the pool of clear, fresh water. The hunter sat down on the bank of the pool and waited to see if the alligator would keep his word.

After spending some time diving in and out of the water and drinking as much as his body could hold, the alligator went out of the pool and walked up to the hunter on the bank. "Thank you very much for taking me to this water. Now I will keep my word and tell you how to become a successful hunter. Go into the woods with your bow and arrows. You will find a tiny doe there, but do not kill it. Do not even shoot at it. Next you will find a large buck. But, again, do not shoot it or kill it. You will later find a large buck that is very old. Shoot this buck. You will easily kill it with your arrows. From then on, you will be able to kill as many deer as you want."

And that is exactly what happened. The hunter followed the instructions of the gator and became one of the most successful hunters of his village.

V. Alligator Miscellany

This final section deals with two Florida cities that benefited from their association with alligators; the gator as mascot; and the word "alligator" in place names.

How an Alligator Sold St. Petersburg
by John Richard Bothwell

This is the true story of how an alligator named Trouble toured far-off places like the Dakotas, Montana, and Washington, promoting St. Petersburg, Florida. This story appeared in Sunrise 200: A Lively Look at St. Petersburg's Past *by John Richard Bothwell (St. Petersburg: Times Publishing Co., 1975, pp. 22–23; reprinted by permission of the publisher).*

There is a small house at 1107 Third Street N in St. Petersburg which does not appear unusual to the passerby—but it is. For there are alligators in the attic and the garage, including the most famous gator of all, Trouble, star of the city's most unique publicity stunt ever.

To be precise, there are alligator heads and hides at the home of Mrs. W. B. "Bill" Carpenter, the lively, talkative widow of a remarkable old-timer whose interests were many.

A genial, good-natured man with a cheerful grin and lively sense of humor, Bill Carpenter helped organize the present-day Board of Realtors and was a member for more than 50 years. His wife was a licensed real estate salesperson for 35 years.

In 1972 the Carpenters felt it was time to close their business. On January 28, 1973, he died at 91, still mentally alert. Chances are he thought a good bit, over the years, about his historic trip with Trouble.

"Bill was twelve when his father, Edward Carpenter, brought the family here from Elm Creek, Nebraska, in 1894, when there were only about two hundred fifty people in St. Petersburg," says Mrs. Carpenter. "His father came here for his health."

A bright, ambitious youngster, Bill promptly got a job as delivery boy for pioneer merchant Ed T. Lewis, who'd arrived in 1888 and later, with one Ed Durant, had opened up a general store on the northeast corner of Third Street and Central Avenue.

"Bill started out driving a wagon, delivering groceries," Mrs. Carpenter recalls. "He'd practice on his horn—he was in the band—as he drove along."

Little gators are so cute!
Credit: Florida State Archives

Almost a decade later, Bill had worked up to bookkeeper. But he had other interests. So he taught his job to a youthful eager beaver, one Ed Wright, who later would become one of Florida's major landowners.

Then Carpenter, in 1905, used his savings to open up a curious enterprise—a combination curio store and movie [theater], the Royal Palm, on Central Avenue between Second and Third Streets, just west of the Detroit Hotel.

"My Bill was always interested in alligators," says his widow fondly. "He had as many as a thousand little alligators in pens back of the store; used to ship them all over the country; used to hatch out the eggs.

"He had a bigger alligator on display in a cage on the sidewalk, by the picture show entrance (children, five cents; adults, ten). I remember he said once a drunken fisherman stuck his hand in and the gator grabbed it. Bill got him out but the man lost his lower arm."

Occasionally, the Royal Palm booked vaudeville. Once a comedian, who knew about the owner's other business, got the scare of his life.

"I had a sixteen-foot live alligator in a room near his dressing room," Carpenter said later, "and this old hound dog that hung around brushed against his leg in a dim light. He thought the alligator had gotten loose. . . ."

The comic is said to have set a new record for leaving a theater.

Adventurous, restless Bill Carpenter sold his curio store and theater after about seven years (1912), and in 1916 hit upon a great idea. Why not see the country, take along a paying asset and advertise St. Petersburg at the same time?

He was rolling in money from his gator-theater profits. He laid out $1,700 for a handsome, well-built four-cylinder Hudson and talked an equally adventurous friend, one Joe Honey, a former sailor, into the project—a motor trip to the Pacific Northwest and California.

Trouble, a 10-year-old, six-foot-long alligator, was to be their mascot and meal ticket. Carpenter correctly figured that the saurian would be a sensation in places like Montana, and he was.

On the morning of June 11, 1916, the two sports rolled out of St. Petersburg, the Hudson loaded to the brim with tents, cooking equipment, rifles, spare tires, bedding, and promotion pamphlets from the Chamber of Commerce.

Atop the pile in a specially-made canvas bag, uneasily scrabbling about, rode Trouble.

Any place they could draw a crowd, the weary saurian would be hauled out. Carpenter would straddle him and get him to show his many teeth as spectators gasped. Then Bill would further amaze all by rubbing Trouble's stomach and "hypnotizing" him, while Joe passed the hat.

Finally, the two pitchmen would pass out St. Petersburg promotional pamphlets, which were resupplied periodically by rail shipment.

At night, Trouble would be staked out by their tent.

The three partners developed sort of an understanding as the weeks passed, Carpenter said later. On one occasion, they freed the alligator on the banks of a river to see just what he'd do, concealing themselves behind some bushes. The gator made no attempt to escape. He merely looked anxiously about for his pals, grunting the creature's distress call.

"An alligator is the dumbest animal in the world," said Carpenter, "but he knows who feeds him."

Blackfoot Indians in the Dakotas were fearful of the creature. Cowboys in Yellowstone Park goggled in amazement. Canadians couldn't believe it. School children marveled.

The tour was a success. But the Hudson was taking a terrible beating from rock-ribbed roads, treacherous, slippery clay, hills, and valleys. Springs and tires were constant casualties.

After limping into Spokane, Washington, the partners agreed they had had enough. If Trouble could have spoken, he surely would have said the same.

They headed back for St. Petersburg, thankful to see palm trees, sand and sunshine again. The four-month trip had covered 14,042 miles. Their bills—mostly for ammunition, gasoline and tires—totaled about $2,000, most of which Trouble had paid for.

The creature was donated to a local alligator farm, but show business had evidently gone to his head. He couldn't get along with the local alligators (bumpkins who had never been out of Pinellas County) and got into nothing but trouble.

Six years later Carpenter got him back and reluctantly shot and skinned him. Trouble's mortal remains still gather dust in the garage at 1107 Third Street N.

How an Alligator Cleaned the Sewers of Tarpon Springs

Mention of this particular alligator appeared in "Remember when an alligator cleaned drains?" 100 Years and Growing, *a supplement to the* Tarpon-Palm Harbor Leader *(June 27, 1987, pp. 3–4). This method of cleaning sewers is not recommended.*

Around the turn of this century, Tarpon Springs was a small town. It had wooden sidewalks, a new sewage system, and no paved streets. A horse-drawn wagon would collect the sewage each night and dispose of it.

In 1910, the man in charge of the water works needed an efficient means to clean the city's drains. What he came up with was certainly a novel idea. He first put a large brush at the end of a long rope. At the other end of the rope, he attached a chain which he put around an alligator's neck. As the alligator made its way through the sewer, his swishing movements enabled the brush to clean up the debris. When he reached the end of the drain pipe, his handler pulled him out. That action of pulling him out also helped clean the pipe.

The Alligator as Mascot
by Kevin M. McCarthy

Several schools and even a minor league baseball team have adopted the gator as a mascot.

Allegheny College in Meadville, Pennsylvania, is a long way from most alligators. How the students chose the gator as the school mascot is an interesting story.

Up through 1925, the school's athletic teams were called the Hilltoppers, Methodists, and the Blue and Gold. However, alliteration won out, and the teams adopted the Allegheny Alligators as their new name.

The new name was helped along in April 1925, when students at the college began publishing a humor magazine called Allegheny Alligator. The editors wrote the following in the first issue of the magazine:

The name, Alligator, was selected not because the alligator is noted for its sense of humor, nor because the haunts of the above-mentioned critter are located in this vicinity, but purely and simply because of the 99.44% alliterative value of its orthography. Then, an alligator has such a stupid, complacent sophistication that he will doubtless feel very much at home among a group of college students.

A column in that first issue was called "Gator Gossip." In the fall of 1926, a new cheerleading type of group, the "Go-Get-'Em Gator Club,"

made its first appearance. Soon after, the college's athletic teams were called the Gators.

San Francisco State University had as its original mascot the Golden Gate Bridge. The school's teams were nicknamed the Gaters, but in time the "e" was transposed into an "o" and the alligator was born. Their trademarked logo has a gator leaning on the Golden Gate Bridge and thus brings together the two concepts.

The student body of the North Campus of **San Jacinto College** in Houston, Texas, voted to have the alligator as their mascot. The other choices were a cheetah and a frontiersman. When the site was being prepared for the campus, workers found alligators living on the site. In the 1990s, there seemed to be only one gator in the area. When the gators become too large, the Texas Parks and Wildlife Department removes and relocates them. The mascot has been painted on the gymnasium wall and on the cooling tower.

Green River Community College in Auburn, Washington, doesn't have many gators around, but the students liked the alliteration of "Green River Gators" enough to choose the gator for their mascot. A woman in the college's nursing program explained the new mascot to her son, who was in

Florida, and he actually sent a live baby gator to his mom. It survived in the mail and was donated by the woman to the college. It was named "GRCC," pronounced "Grick" for Green River Community College, and kept in an incubator in the Student Center. He didn't like the cold weather and would be found from time to time curled up next to a heat register, but he survived.

Later, a dean kept the reptile in his basement and would feed it pieces of meat on a stick until a new hothouse was finished on the campus. Everyone looked forward to the day that the hothouse would be finished because then the heat could be adjusted to Grick's content. On the day the hothouse was finished and Grick was placed in his new home, he died.

Tacoma Community College felt bad for Green River Community College and bought the school another gator, but it died before it ever made it to its new home. Then, a man in a nearby tavern won a gator in a contest and donated it to Green River on condition that the reptile's name be "kegger." Kegger made it to a few games, but he too expired. The college then decided not to replace the gator, but it has kept the mascot in its emblem.

T he **University of Florida** began using a gator for its mascot back in 1907. At that time, Phillip Miller, who owned a stationery store in Gainesville, Florida, was visiting his son at the University of Virginia in Charlottesville. When he tried to order some University of Florida pennants there to sell in Gainesville, Miller suggested the alligator for two reasons: First, no other school at that time had an alligator as a mascot; and second, the reptile was native to Florida.

When the pennant maker admitted that he had never seen an alligator and could therefore not design one for the pennants, Miller's son went to the local library, found a picture of a gator in a book, and presented a copy to the pennant maker. When the pennants arrived in Gainesville in time for the 1908 football season, the blue banners had on them a large orange alligator—and a mascot was born.

Among the nonacademic institutions that use the alligator as a mascot are the **Norwich Navigators**, a double-A minor league affiliate of the New York Yankees located in Yantic, Connecticut. The word "gator" appears in "navigator," hence the alligator mascot.

In 1995, one thousand children entered a contest to name the mascot, suggesting such names as Alli the Alligator, Al, Chomper, Termi-Gator, and Wally Gator. The winner was Tater, chosen because "tater" rhymes with "alligator" and is also slang for a home run.

Place Names with "Alligator"
by Kevin M. McCarthy

According to *Omni Gazetteer of the United States of America* (1991), 160 different place names have "alligator" in them, ranging from streams (108), lakes (59), and swamps (20) to a rock (1), school (1), harbor (1), pond (1), and reef (1). Twenty-seven states have an "alligator" place name. Florida (63), Texas (48), Louisiana (40), and North Carolina (30) lead the way, and several states have just one "alligator": Alaska, Idaho, Iowa, Kentucky, Nevada, New Jersey, New Mexico, New York, Oklahoma, Oregon, Wisconsin, and Wyoming.

There's a negative connotation associated with the word "alligator." The town of Alligator, Florida, which was named after Seminole Chief Alligator, changed its name to Lake City after a number of its citizens found the name of the reptile distasteful as a place name. A member of the Legislature in Tallahassee facetiously tried to have the name changed to "Crocodile," but that effort failed.

George R. Stewart, in his book *Names on the Land* (1945, p. 117), points out that the name "alligator" is seldom given to places where people live, but only to out-of-the-way places. It could be that people prefer names of warm, cuddly animals for the places where they live— for example, Cat Island, Deer Creek, and Manatee River, all in Florida— rather than of fierce reptiles.

One of the most famous roads in Florida crosses the southern part of the state from Andytown (near Fort Lauderdale) on the east coast to Naples on the west coast. The 84-mile-long tollway was supposed to have been called "The Everglades Parkway," but when one of the people opposed to its construction remarked, "Only alligators would use that road," its unofficial name was born: "Alligator Alley."

Florida Fun Facts by Eliot Kleinberg. At last—a collection of every fact, large and small, that you need to know about Florida. Answers to questions like: What's bigger, Lake Okeechobee or Rhode Island? What's wrong with Citrus County's name? And hundreds more! *ISBN 1-56164-068-9*

The Florida Reader:Visions of Paradise edited by Maurice O'Sullivan and Jack Lane. Selections in this collection of stories and essays about Florida range from tales of adventures among Native Americans by the Spanish Gentleman of Elvas to the short stories of Marjorie Kinnan Rawlings, from the romantic reflections of William Bartram and Silvia Sunshine to the carefully crafted prose of Zora Neale Hurston and John Muir. *ISBN 1-56164-062-X*

Forever Island and *Allapattah* in one volume by Patrick Smith. *Forever Island* has been called the classic novel of the Everglades. *Allapattah* is the story of a young Seminole in despair in the white man's world. *ISBN 0-910923-42-6*

Legends of the Seminoles by Betty Mae Jumper. This collection of rich, spoken tales—written down for the first time—impart valuable lessons about living in harmony with nature and about why the world is the way it is. Each story is illustrated with an original painting by Guy LaBree. *ISBN 1-56164-040-9*

Tellable Cracker Tales collected by Annette Bruce. Memorable characters from Florida history come alive in these folktales and legends, tall tales, and gator tales. Pull up your favorite chair and a few listeners and start your own storytelling tradition with the gems in this collection. *ISBN 1-56164-094-8*